NIGHT SKYY

RICH BULLOCK

REDDING, CALIFORNIA

Book cover design by Robert Henslin

Published by RichWords Press, USA

v 4/5/24

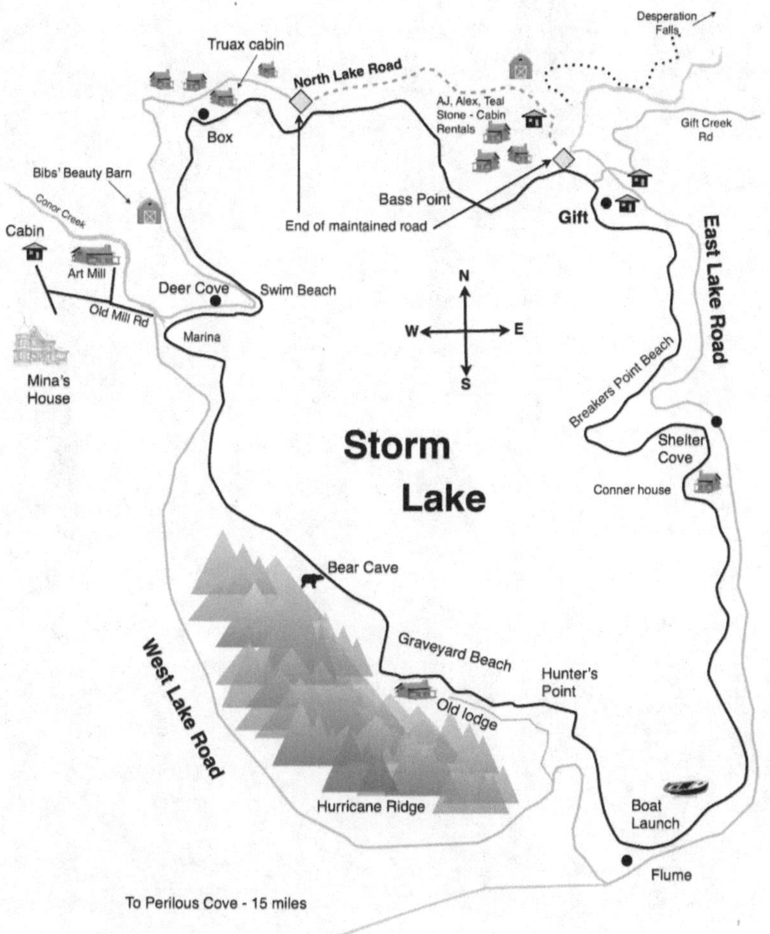

Desperation Falls
Truax cabin
North Lake Road
AJ, Alex, Teal Stone - Cabin Rentals
Gift Creek Rd
Box
Bibs' Beauty Barn
Bass Point
Conor Creek
End of maintained road
Gift
Cabin
Art Mill
East Lake Road
Deer Cove
Swim Beach
N
Old Mill Rd
W
E
Marina
S
Mina's House
Breakers Point Beach
Storm Lake
Shelter Cove
Conner house
Bear Cave
Graveyard Beach
Hunter's Point
West Lake Road
Old lodge
Boat Launch
Hurricane Ridge
Flume
To Perilous Cove - 15 miles

NIGHT SKYY

WRITINGS OF V.M. NARRANO

Our deepest desire is to love and be loved in a way that risks everything.

We don't choose our destiny any more than we design it. Our role is to embrace it when it slaps us in the face.

Life is full of choices. Make one.
If it doesn't work out, make a better one.

CHAPTER 1

"Hi, all. Skyy D here, and you're listening to *Night Thoughts* on Black Owl Radio. I hope you're having a good evening. Thanks for dropping in for my ramblings and to hear some great music from independent artists all over the world."

Skyy Delaney perused the comments and questions already rolling in on her show's comments page. Would *Creeper* show up tonight? Especially considering the topic. She and Big Jerry at Black Owl blocked him every way imaginable, but he always got the first comment through—sometimes more. He'd only missed one show in ten weeks.

"Two days until Valentine's Day, and love is in the air. Or at least you'd think so from all the red candy boxes in drug stores. What's up with that, anyway? Do any women pack away that much chocolate? I'd have zits the size of quarters and weigh 400 pounds. But that's a topic I'll save for another night."

Someone in comments asked how to find the music she featured, and she posted the links in a public comment visible to all who were online. Others requested specific songs or bands. Those she copied to a separate note window. But now that she'd mentioned Valentine's Day, most comments turned to relationships.

"BillyTJ wants to know my favorite chocolate. That would be the kind I don't have to exercise off at the gym. Send me a box of those."

Skyy's broadcast "studio" for her Internet radio show consisted of a laptop, microphone, and the dining table in her rented Tucson guest house. To reduce sound reflection, she'd spread two cheap mover's blankets on the tile floor and draped two more across the table and over the remaining dining chair. Best she could do on her budget.

She pulled her new, Blue Yeti microphone closer. It made her voice sound full and sultry—at least, that's what reviewers said.

"As we think about love and relationships, I want to read you a quote I heard a couple of years ago that changed my life. Here it is:

> *'There comes a time in a man's life when he asks himself three questions:*
>
> *Do I want to stay in this job?*
>
> *Do I want to live in this place?*
>
> *Do I want to stay with this woman?'"*

The quote had played on the car radio while Skyy drove to the grocery store with her then boyfriend. She fought a frown before continuing.

"The experts undoubtedly thought those questions applied to a fifty-year-old balding guy with a paunch who decides to sell his sensible Honda sedan and buy a sports car. A *convertible* sports car. I thought so too.

"Loser Boyfriend in the passenger seat next to me wasn't even thirty years old, yet he asked himself those questions and decided the answer to each was *no*. Within three days, he quit his job, cleared his stuff out of our apartment, and left for Florida to quote, '*live on a boat*.' He took our rescue puppy, but I wasn't invited."

That happened a week before Valentine's Day two years ago. She held the mute button while exhaling a cleansing breath. *Let it go*. Yet it still stung.

"But listen to this, ladies: this is the important part, and it's just for you. After a few days of sobbing in bed, I got up, slapped myself twice—the red marks lasted till the next day —and took an ice-cold shower while blasting Lana Del Rey on my Bluetooth speaker.

"The thing about a cold shower is," Skyy leaned into her mic, "you aren't thinking about your torn heart when you're freezing your butt off and yelling like a crazy woman."

She paused, envisioning her listeners turning up the volume for her next words. "Get this, girls: it's *your* butt and *your* crazy, not his. No one else makes you whole. It's up to you."

Skyy clicked on a music file, triggering Big Jerry's slow fade-in option. "Okay, you guys out there, you can join back in. Hope you learned something. Now let's listen to a new set of songs from Slide3 out of the Village in New York. Their album is *Gremlin Candy*."

The stagnant air in her tiny room was beyond stifling, but she couldn't use the noisy AC unit in the middle of a live show. She resorted to draping a wet towel around her neck and mopping her brow with a washcloth. Tucson in winter. She shook her head.

More Valentine's questions—and a few best wishes for her —filled the scrolling window.

Then a chill crawled up her spine. A comment from *Creeper*.

I'd love to see you in the shower. We could—

Skyy deleted the comment before her eyes could read the rest of the pervert's slime. She'd made that mistake before. Deleting a comment was much easier than erasing lingering mental images. Her fingers fumbled the keys as she composed a message to Big Jerry that *Creeper* got through their blocks—again.

But dwelling on the breach now wasn't possible. The rest of the show flew by in an avalanche of questions, comments, and exciting plans for *"The Best Valentine's Ev-ver!!!"* Tons of exclamation marks; heart emojis too. Skyy read the best of them aloud, relaxing again in the positive flow. The few that sent emojis of a bloody dagger were innocent and made her laugh. At least some people agreed with her dissing of Cupid's big holiday.

Then one rolled up that again stopped her smile.

Maybe someone will buy me a Valentine's gift someday. I don't care what it is. - ***K***

This wasn't the first post from K, but it was the first that more than hinted K was female—and probably young if she'd never had a Valentine's gift. On the surface, the words could be interpreted as hopeful, but Skyy read doubt and discouragement in every one of K's messages, this one included.

While the Black Owl Radio program site allowed for direct responses to posts, Skyy rarely did so. And unless K replied, there was no way to know if K received it. Still, she had to try.

K. I wish I could help. - ***Skyy D***

That was the frustration of being virtual—she could only encourage, not touch. K could be across town or thousands of miles away. For once, she'd like to really help someone.

She mopped her forehead as the final song ended and the show clock counted down toward the end of the hour.

"That was 'Blue Crazy' by Wint. I love her stuff. And if *you* liked the music featured tonight, please stream or buy it. Support these great artists.

"Unfortunately, that's all the time we have tonight. Don't forget to follow me on Black Owl Radio. If you create a login, you can leave comments, listen to the show live on your mobile app, and keep up with all the *Night Thoughts* latest. I'll talk to you next Tuesday.

"Remember: be safe—and don't stay up too late unless you're listening to *Night Thoughts*."

Canon Truax removed his earbuds and closed the Black Owl Radio phone app before the next show's intro intruded on the experience that was Skyy D.

While he appreciated her efforts to promote talented artists who weren't part of the commercial music business, *she* was why he tuned in. Her voice was a burgundy silk scarf drifting across the night sky.

"What are you grinning at, bro?" Canon's brother, Martin, dropped onto the second chaise on the cabin's front porch. "Yikes. This vinyl is like ice." He squirmed around, warming up the cushion with friction. It was far colder than last night when they hauled the old lounges outside.

"Clear sky makes for cold air," Canon said, staring at the colorful splash of brilliant pinpricks painted against the blackness of space above Storm Lake, California.

"You've been listening to that Internet chick again, haven't you?" Mart said. "Next you'll be writing poems to the moon and talking about mauve fabrics. For a tough cop, you're getting sappy."

Canon laughed. "You don't even know what color mauve is, bro. And you have to admit, she has the sexiest voice you ever heard."

"Not much you can do about it. She could be anywhere in the world, so it's not as if you'll bump into her at the grocery store here or home."

"Nah, she's closer than that. I've got a feeling."

"Yeah? Well, *I've* got a feeling we'd better get some sleep. The fish bite at dawn, and that's in"—he pressed the stem of his watch—"less than six hours. If you aren't up, I'm going by myself." He levered up off the chaise.

"I'll be right in," Canon said to Mart's retreating back, then turned his gaze to the lake. On still nights it reflected the brighter stars like an obsidian dance floor, but tonight a light breeze rippled the surface enough to wash away the pinpoints. Even yard lights on the occupied cabins across the lake cast no reflections. Every night was different, and each beautiful in its own way.

Since their parents died, he and Mart tried to get together at Storm Lake two or three times a year. It had been tough lately, what with Mart being hired full time by the Salinas Fire Department, and Canon's temporary assignment to the Sheriff's drug task force in San Diego County.

Mart viewed the cabin as a vacation house, somewhere to bring friends and do some fishing. But for Canon, the cabin was solace in a crazy world, a place more home than anywhere else.

"Where are you, Skyy D?" Although some of the other Black Owl Radio hosts posted pictures and some personal information on their profile pages, Skyy D never did. There was info about upcoming show topics, links referenced during a program, and the occasional poll, but nothing of her current surroundings or recent travels. She never mentioned local venues or geographical landmarks.

Canon almost laughed, because her online presence was more secretive than his. Perhaps it was basic caution, a hedge against potential stalkers. Of course, it was possible she was former law enforcement who knew, like he did, it was safer not to reveal personal information. However, he couldn't help wondering if there was an incident somewhere in her past. Was she running? Hiding?

The sole clue to her identity was her voice. Mart would give him grief if he knew how much time Canon spent analyzing each nuance of pronunciation. But no matter how many times he listened, no accent or pattern of regionalisms stood out.

Tonight, though, he detected a brush of sadness in her voice when she signed off. It was slight, but there, as if something happened right before the end of the show.

He clicked the Black Owl page and composed a message.

Heard your show tonight. Ouch. Kind of harsh, don't you think? I mean, not all men are thoughtless clods. Not all men leave. Many are good guys, like my brother. Others are great—like me. :-)

Canon thought again of the tone of her sign-off.

*As I said last time, I'm a cop. So if you ever need anything, or if you'd like to talk or meet, you know where to reach me. Have a good night, Skyy D. Catch you next week. - **Canon***

He tapped the post button, feeling a strange combination of teenage foolishness and hope. Suggesting a meeting or talking was far bolder than he'd been in previous messages, and he hoped it didn't sound too stalkerish. He'd given her his Facebook profile, locked down as it was, as an offering that he was for real, but she had yet to reply to any of his messages. Still, there was no gain if he never tried.

Other than Loser Boyfriend, she never mentioned anyone special, not even family or friends. From her familiarity with the indie music scene and her style of speech and word choice, he thought her under thirty years old. Beyond that—tall, short, fat, thin, ugly, gorgeous—he had no idea.

The stiff vinyl creaked as he peeled himself off the chair and stood. Dawn would be even colder than it was now, yet he welcomed the recurring routine: the familiar *thunk* and squeak of their tennis shoes on the aluminum boat bottom, the whispered comments that carried clear across to the far shore in the predawn silence, the splashes of scarred wooden oars disturbing the calm water.

They would glide through foot-high mist pulled up from the surface as the sun hinted through tall pines. And when they reached one of their favorite spots, the creak of wicker creels handed down from their father's father signaled the coming challenge. All the smells and sounds—all the senses, really—from hundreds of trips beginning when they were little boys, were etched into his and Mart's souls. More than hooking a trout or bass, being on the water with family was important to who he was.

The screen door hinges complained when he pulled it open. Another reminder of his childhood—and that his parents left this world far too soon. There would be no more fishing trips with his father.

Far out in the darkness, a bird called, perhaps seeking

companionship. Canon paused, listening. None of its kind answered.

He pushed open the inside door, easing the screen door shut behind.

> *Hey, Skyy D. How about going fishing with me at dawn sometime? - **Canon***

He sent the new message and headed to bed, smiling at the snarky response he hoped would come.

CHAPTER 2

Too early Wednesday morning, Skyy swung her legs out of bed, no longer able to tolerate the sun beating through the thin curtains. She wouldn't be surprised if they burst into flame, because she was about to.

Opening the window wasn't an option. The 95-degree heat already had the window AC in the living area *burrat-tat-tatting* like a truck's Jake brakes on a steep downhill grade. The poor unit would probably have a literal meltdown when summer heat arrived.

Of all the places she'd lived around the country, Tucson was... Well, she didn't want to go there. Or *stay*, for that matter. This was February. It should be cold, snow on the cactus or something. And according to grocery store checkout clerks, that's the way it normally was. This year was *unseasonably warm*, they said. Plain old hot was more accurate.

Arizona had seemed like a good idea when she lived in Louisiana smacking bugs every two seconds and breathing air the consistency of salty Jell-O. She hadn't lasted long there, especially after her disastrous trip to find her brother.

Hungry but too tired to think about fixing food, she flopped down at the dining table and opened her laptop to the *Night Thoughts* site. Over 154,000 subscribers, up nearly a thousand since last night's show. Two years ago she'd been at fifty-two. *Just* fifty-two—not thousand.

"Wow. That's amazing."

Talking to herself didn't bother her as much as it had right after Loser Boyfriend left for Florida, although one-sided conversations were a nagging reminder she had no one with whom to share life, not even a pet or dead plant.

But virtual friends were better than no friends. She pulled her laptop closer. There were dozens of comments on past shows and several private direct messages. Not unusual.

She scrolled to the bottom of the DMs and began with the oldest. Two were from legitimate radio stations. Now that she was gaining a following, they were offering her a spot in their lineups. Flattering, but she had no interest. They'd lure you in, then begin dictating content and strapping on demands. Soon she'd be trapped, another *whatever's-popular* copycat. She scrolled up the list of messages until one coaxed her lips into a smile.

Canon Truax.

She clicked and read the message. Three times.

He thought she was harsh on guys? She laughed. He obviously hadn't heard her shows soon after Loser Boyfriend left her behind. She considered herself downright mellow now.

Canon Truax had sent messages after most of her last twenty or so shows, and it annoyed her that each week she anticipated his message more than the week before. If he missed a week, her disappointment annoyed her even more. Not that she ever replied. Lessons learned early on.

When *Night Thoughts* first began, she used Facebook and other social media to interface with fans. It quickly got out of hand, requiring constant deleting of hateful, sometimes vile, posts. The first freak who suggested what he'd like to do to her weirded her out so much she'd cancelled her next show and triple-checked her privacy settings on every platform.

All the Black Owl DJs had the same problems, so Big Jerry set up an internally monitored page for each show on the site. A simple mobile app soon followed, providing listeners with show interaction, live streaming, topic suggestions and polls, plus direct messages. Even with the new system, Skyy kept her real identity and location secret, and regularly blocked strangers who contacted her.

But she hadn't blocked Canon Truax.

And there was a second message from him that had her laughing. *Fishing at dawn.* Seriously? Morning was not her best time. And fish guts and bait? She shuddered.

He'd sent her his Facebook link last week, and she switched over to it to see if there was anything new. Talk about all American guy. Good looking, her age or close. His profile was sparse; nothing about being in law enforcement like in his direct message. She figured that was for his own safety. He never mentioned people by name, and his friends list was private. But there were photos.

Oh, were there photos. Body surfing in the Pacific Ocean were her favorites, especially one of him striding out of the waves in low-slung swim shorts. If she had the high-quality original, she could sell wall posters to teenage girls on her stores and make a fortune. Other pictures showed Canon holding a string of five fish with a lake in the background, Canon with a man who resembled him standing beside a smoking grill, and Canon tubing behind a motorboat.

Then there was that one pic, the one that kept her from blocking his messages on Black Owl: a profile shot of him staring across a sky-blue lake. She zoomed in like she had a dozen times before. Dark hair cut short, square jaw shadowed with a day's growth, and a sadness in the lines at the corner of his eye. The creases and shadows spoke of pain or loss, and it made her want to know more. Made her want to know *him*.

There were other pictures: riding four-wheelers, posing in khaki shorts and hiking boots by a Sequoia National Park trail marker, waterskiing, and diving off a floating wooden platform.

She switched back to the beach scenes. Actual abs. Wow.

So if you ever need anything, or if you'd like to talk or meet, you know where to reach me.

Her finger slid the cursor to the Black Owl direct message window, hovering above the reply button. Should she? Big Jerry had good firewalls, so it wasn't like he could find her through the app. Not unless he had a warrant out on her.

Her cell phone rang and she jumped, convinced it was the cop calling—maybe to arrest her for…well, stalking his page or something.

"Hello?" she said cautiously.

"Hola, Skyy. You had breakfast yet? This place is dead."

Skyy relaxed. Lupe Rivera was her closest friend in Tucson—almost her *only* friend—and owner of Miss Lupe's Mexican restaurant that catered to locals.

"Hey, Lupe. Got anything good today?"

The woman laughed. "It's *all* good."

"Be there in a few." She closed her laptop and ducked under the entry into her bathroom to shower off the morning sticky.

Her landlord's ad had touted the rental as *"A quaint backyard bungalow, complete with bedroom, kitchen, and bathroom."* He was also a visionary with deeply tinted rose glasses.

The structure was two, big-box store garden sheds shoved together with the connecting walls cut out. Two hundred eighty-eight square feet of luxury living. Plumbing? Yes. Insulation? Not so much. Skyy squeezed into the plastic shower stall—so tiny she had to step out if she dropped the soap—and adjusted the water temperature as cool as she dared.

Usually, she loved experiencing different parts of the country, getting a sense of the culture, sampling the local cuisine, even picking up show ideas by eavesdropping in local coffee shops. And no one could deny the beauty of the desert at night with zillions of stars overhead. But almost from day one the desert didn't feel right. Half a year and she was ready to see the next place.

She dressed in shorts and a T-shirt proclaiming *I ♥ saguaro*. Simple wardrobe options were one good thing about living where summer got an early start…or never left. After a quick brush of her teeth and hair, she slid her feet into flip-flops and headed out into the broiler morning.

Her Jeep Cherokee's door handle was basking in full sun, so she used the hem of her T-shirt to tug it open. Fortunately, the car had cloth seats. She started the engine and got the AC going.

In a New Year's resolution to be truthful with herself, she admitted her restlessness wasn't only from Tucson's heat or the simple desire to see somewhere new. She could no longer deny her growing desire to find permanence, develop roots she'd never known, never sought, never imagined she wanted. Until now.

Was it the cop and his friendly messages? His beautiful lake? In all her landings across the U.S., she instinctively knew each place was temporary, a consumable experience of new things before moving on. They were all impetuous choices. *Intentionally* searching for a specific place—or maybe a specific person—was something new.

"Hola, Skyy," Lupe said as Skyy entered the restaurant. Two men in work clothes and straw cowboy hats glanced up from their plates and Skyy traded nods of recognition. They were regulars, too, and the only other patrons.

Soon after Skyy arrived in Tucson, she'd gotten lost on backstreets and stopped to ask directions from a woman weeding the flowerbed in front of a house-turned-restaurant. The gardener was Lupe, and she invited Skyy inside for homemade tortillas. Two hours later, she had a new friend and a leftover container loaded with the best Mexican food she'd ever tasted.

Although Lupe was only half-Mexican and hailed from Oregon, she had assimilated the local culture so thoroughly Skyy doubted many knew she wasn't born and raised in the Southwest. That's what twenty-five years in a place would do. Skyy knew nothing of that.

"Good morning, Lupe," Skyy said, breathing in red sauce, tortillas, salsa, and beans. She let her growling stomach lead her to a stool at the low counter separating the dining area from the kitchen. Lupe had a cup of coffee waiting before Skyy got settled.

"Thanks for calling." She blew across the hot brew, the robust aroma giving the day more promise. "I'm starving."

"Of course you are." Lupe delivered a plate heaped with chorizo scrambled eggs, beans, and rice. "You don't eat enough." She came around the counter with her own mug of coffee and sat beside Skyy.

"Don't hold back," Skyy said, taking an embarrassingly large bite. The flavors exploded in her mouth, and she had to close her eyes and breathe through the experience. It never got old. "Wow, this is so good."

"Sí, gracias." Lupe sipped her coffee, then said, "You look bad. What's wrong."

"Sheesh, Lupe. *Really* don't hold back." She rubbed her cheeks. Did she have pillowcase creases? Maybe a little more looking in the mirror before going out next time.

Lupe waved off the comment, waiting while Skyy finished another bite. "So…?"

With a sigh—and not from the fantastic food—Skyy set down her fork. "I'm not sure Tucson's the place for me," she said, then felt guilty for dissing her friend's town.

"What are you looking for?" Lupe asked, then gestured for Skyy to keep eating while she rose to cash out the two men who had finished their breakfasts.

For some reason, the question irritated her. Maybe she was looking for some place where not everything in her bathroom had to be travel size? That would be a nice change, wouldn't it? But if she was truthful, she had an underlying fear that her life, not just her toiletries, had become tiny.

She was mopping up the last red sauce with a flour tortilla when Lupe returned from chatting with the men. They left, and she and Lupe had the place to themselves.

"What makes you think I'm looking for something?"

Lupe narrowed her eyes. "If you'd found it, you'd be there instead of living in the desert complaining of the heat. Right?"

Skyy nearly laughed at the simplicity. "Was that the way it was for you? Coming here felt like the right place?" Lupe nodded, but Skyy noted the way her friend hunched over the counter, as if a weight rested on her shoulders too.

"So, my friend Skyy, where are you going this time?"

Instead of talking about the cop and his lake in California, Skyy asked, "Is there something wrong, Lupe?" Was she upset that Skyy was thinking of moving?

Lupe sipped her coffee and stared through the service window into the kitchen area. There was a man working in the back who Skyy hadn't seen before.

"I've spent half of my life in Tucson, most of it right here in this restaurant." She turned to Skyy. "I've cleaned the ceilings, walls, and floors, and every piece of equipment, glass, and silverware too many times to count. The restaurant business is long hours, hard work, and it never ends. And all for a chance at not going under."

Skyy knew about being financially close to the edge, but she couldn't imagine being tied to one place every day of the week, year on year.

"Do you enjoy it?" Skyy asked.

Lupe looked around the room and gave a rueful smile. "For a long time, yes. Less so lately."

"Your daughter?" Skyy asked. Lupe's daughter and family moved to Florida two years ago.

"I really miss those grandkids," Lupe said. Then she sat up straight. "That's why I called you today. I was hoping you could come so I could tell you. I've decided to sell and move to Florida."

"You…" Skyy opened, then closed her mouth. "What?" She'd eaten here at least twice a week for months. Lupe not being behind the counter seemed…wrong.

"I've been restless," the woman said, tilted her mug in Skyy's direction. "Much like you, my friend. That's why I asked you what you are looking for. For me, I've figured it out. Family is more important than working twelve-hour days."

"But… What will you do there?" Skyy tried to picture Lupe in any other setting.

Her friend shrugged. "Lots of old retired ladies live in Florida. Maybe work in a yarn or quilting store. Definitely not the restaurant business. Or I'll just lie on the beach for a few months and listen to the ocean. Drink Mai Tais."

Quilts and fruity cocktails? "When are you thinking of moving?"

Lupe shook her head. "No thinking. Doing. The restaurant sale closed yesterday afternoon. I didn't want to mention it to you or anyone until it was a sure thing. My moving truck comes next Wednesday."

"Lupe, I don't know what to say, except I'll miss you." Skyy blinked at the sudden moisture in her eyes. Her friend was leaving in a week.

Lupe gave Skyy's hand a squeeze, then pulled her into a hug. "Here's what I say to *you,* my friend Skyy: Life goes quickly, so go find what you desire. You shouldn't live it alone."

Saying goodbye to Lupe left Skyy more than slightly depressed. London Grammar's *Truth Is a Beautiful Thing* was probably too melancholy, but the music fit her mood while she worked her other business.

She'd developed a knack for figuring out what people wanted before they knew, and her targeted ads on various social media sites kept the orders flowing into her multiple online stores, all of which were under the banner of *SkyyRiver*. She had *SkyyRiver Toys, SkyyRiver Home,* and *SkyyRiver Electronics*.

Although everything shipped straight to customers from suppliers, service problems landed squarely in her lap. Today's issue was missed delivery dates by one supplier, and she couldn't afford poor reviews. She buckled down and fired off an email to the supplier and apology messages to the customers. That done, she began setting up new ad campaigns.

The work was another reminder that life these days was virtual. People met, fell in love, and broke up electronically—sometimes without ever meeting. Last week, a caller told about how she'd had a baby with a man she met on a dating site. That wasn't the odd part. A clinic froze his sperm, then flew it to her doctor's office for implantation. She became pregnant and gave birth without the father ever knowing where she lived, nor did they know each other's last names. It was like using an anonymous donor from a sperm bank, except Daddy wasn't entirely anonymous, just unmet.

So not what Skyy wanted for her own life. The more she talked to people online, the more she longed for normal, for old-fashioned one-on-one.

That got her thinking about Canon Truax, and she brought up his messages from last night again.

So if you ever need anything, or if you'd like to talk or meet, you know where to reach me.

What if he was a normal person looking for that same one-on-one?

Hand trembling a little, she clicked in the message reply window and typed *Good morning,* then frowned at it.

That sounded… like she'd just woken up beside him in bed. She pounded the delete button until the letters disappeared.

Ignoring him was the safest thing, but the idea of sending a message had taken root. She couldn't just leave and go buy toilet paper at Target or something. His after-show messages these last weeks felt like a connection, even if it was across the ether and so far entirely one-sided. He didn't know she read them and waited for his next one. If she never replied, he might give up.

And what if, like he said, he *was* one of the good guys? Could she not take the chance? Could she go on with her luxurious life of rented garden-shed-guest-houses in paradise locales like Tucson?

Recognizing the sudden inspiration, she changed screens and jotted notes in her Show Topics document: *Where to live. Have you ever moved just to go somewhere new? What matters in making the decision?* Then she switched back to the messaging screen.

Her fingers twitched over the keys for two full minutes, mentally composing and discarding message after message before finally typing two words.

*Hi. - **Skyy***

Before she could overthink it, she hit the Return key.

Instantly, her heartbeat sped up, and she brushed perspiration off her upper lip with the back of her hand.

"Oh, crap. What have I done?" Rarely had she contacted a fan. And this time she hadn't added the D like she always did for her professional persona. *Skyy* without the *D* sounded personal, friendly, stripped down. She was *always* Skyy D, the professional radio personality to her fans—all 154,000 of them. But now to one person she was just Skyy.

And she should have said more. Instead of wording that would close the conversation, such as *thanks for listening,* this sounded like an invitation, an opening for him to jump in.

What if he was a creeper like *Creeper*?

CHAPTER 3

SKYY SPENT THURSDAY MORNING WORRYING ABOUT HER MESSAGE to Canon Truax and contemplating a move. Lupe's final words haunted her: *Life goes quickly, so go find what you desire. You shouldn't live it alone.*

Did that mean finding a certain cop?

The *bungalow slash garden shed* shared the utilities and Wi-Fi with the main house, so moving simply required informing her landlord, Troy. Her rent was paid through February, and her deposit covered her last month. That meant she didn't have to move immediately, but now that she'd gotten her teeth into the idea, she couldn't let it go.

Where to land next was the pressing question. Guest houses and garage conversions were best. They provided privacy and freedom to work or sleep anytime she chose. No toilets flushing in the next room, no dog barking in the hall.

Problem was, both types of rentals were rare, and many were occupied by jobless sons and daughters who moved home after college. Either that or else the owners jumped on the Airbnb wagon to generate extra bucks. Skyy earned enough to live on if she was careful, but she couldn't compete with those high Airbnb nightly rates.

She searched the Internet and called on listings in Flagstaff and Prescott. Neither met her needs or price. Although she loved the thought of living on water, especially after the desert, Lake Havasu City proved ridiculously expensive—and was probably hotter than Tucson.

Lakes dotted the upper Midwest, and she could find something there—once the snows melted. Going from frying pan to freezer wasn't a good move. And they had a lot of bugs there. She sighed. The older she got, the pickier she became about weather and location. She'd become a weather snob.

No, the truth was that none of these other cities lived up to Canon Truax staring across his California lake.

And why hadn't he messaged her back? She grabbed her phone again to check. It had been a whole day. Was he surprised by her message, put off? After all, he had no idea what she looked like, how old she was, or if she was a convicted felon, con artist, or international jewel thief. Well, jewel thief might be a stretch, but as a cop, he'd be cautious by training.

"Skyy?" The door opened without a knock, and a spiky head of hair poked around the edge in a blast of hot noon sun. The rest of Ember Peyron clomped inside when she spotted Skyy at the table.

Ember—her real name was Sally, which she *"detested"*—described herself as *"half black, half white, and half alien."* The otherworldly part came in the hairdo which changed colors every week or so. Today it was black blending to purple at mid-length and tipped in pink.

"Nice earrings," Skyy said. They were silver-wrapped jade, finished with feathers that matched her hair color, and so long they brushed her shoulders. "They go good with…"

"Nothing!" Ember laughed, closing the door.

Her go-to wardrobe was a variety of bright Spandex tank tops, clashing shorts, and black lace-up boots. The overall effect was petite Goth meets Southwest in the Caribbean. Silver eye shadow on her mocha skin made her eyes appear enormous.

Skyy wondered if she could rock multiple ear piercings like Ember did, but drew the line at the nostril ring. Not happening. If there were other body mods on the girl, they weren't visible. Skyy pictured Ember as typical of those who listened to her midnight radio show.

Proudly eighteen *"and a twelfth"*—although Skyy thought the girl looked a couple years younger—Ember lived nearby in a group transition home for kids who aged out of the foster system.

"I'm on my own with nowhere to go," she announced the first time they met. That wasn't technically true, because Ember had flagged Skyy down on the street and asked for a ride to the mall, standing in front of the car until Skyy raised her hands in surrender. It seemed the teen always had somewhere to go.

"What's up?" Ember asked, sliding into the chair beside Skyy and checking out the computer screen. "Ooh, pretty lake."

Before Sky could react, Ember tapped the arrow key and Canon Truax's photo filled the screen. The one of him walking out of the surf. The abs pic. The one she—

"Holy cra—"

"Language, young lady," Skyy broke in, snapping her computer shut.

Ember picked up Skyy's diet soda and took a swig. "Who's the hottie?"

Skyy pushed away from the table and stood, abandoning

her drink. Ember opened the laptop and clicked through the pictures of Canon.

"Wow. Name?"

"Canon."

"Oh, yeah, I see it here. Truax." She clicked through his profile. "What's he do?"

"He says he's a cop." Skyy opened the refrigerator and got another Orange Crush.

"A cop hottie?" Ember waggled a finger between Canon's photo and Skyy and raised a brow.

Skyy stared at the floor and shook her head. "He's only a listener." Ember was one of the few people on Earth who knew Skyy Delaney was Skyy D of *Night Thoughts*. She still wasn't sure how Ember wrestled that information from her before they even got to the mall that day. The girl had a way.

"There's nothing on his profile about being a cop," Ember said. "Are you sure?"

"Well, not positive, but that's what he said in his message."

Ember's eyebrows rose along with her voice. "You're messaging with him?"

"Only once." She hated how defensive it sounded. "Yesterday morning."

"You never talk with anyone off-air."

"I know, but..." For some reason, Skyy told her all she knew about Canon. The girl was like being wired to a lie detector.

Ember turned back to the screen, scrolling through the pictures again. "Where is this?"

"Somewhere in California. He doesn't say where."

"Ooh, a man of mystery." Ember's expression flashed from fun to guarded. "Are you going there?"

"Well..."

"Take me with you."

Skyy looked up. "What? Ember, I can't just... I mean, I don't even know where—"

"You should go meet him. And take me." Ember finished the drink and crinkled the can like she always did. She set it rocking on the table beside the computer as she rose. "I'm working till nine tonight. I've gotta go." With that, she was out the door.

Skyy sank onto the vacated chair, the room still alive with the teen's energy. As tough as Ember came across, insecurity shimmered right below the surface. She had no family, no one to ground her, to protect her. At eighteen she was legally an adult, and everything she did in life from now on was totally up to her—alone. How could anyone survive at that age? The system wasn't fair.

Skyy knew the feeling. Although her brother, Vance, was still alive somewhere, she, too, felt alone in the world. And as bad as the fiasco with Loser Boyfriend turned out, at least Skyy hadn't been by herself for the time it lasted. She had to admit, the breakup strengthened her. Still, there were times—especially when facing a new town or city—when the enormity of the universe shook her to the core. Her one-woman life raft drifting on the endless ocean could spring a leak any moment. Then what would she do?

But regardless of Ember's insistence, Skyy couldn't just go chasing across the country after some guy she'd said literally one word to. She might hunt all over California and never find him. Or she *might* find him and then what?

She could just ask him where he lived. That's what Ember would do.

No. She stood and paced the few feet of floor space in the room. That wasn't happening. A few messages didn't make for a relationship. She needed to concentrate on her work.

Maybe message Truax more and get to know him before doing something ridiculous such as meeting him. And Ember needed to stay in the group home until she got established in a more permanent living situation.

Despite her resolve, a few minutes later she found herself checking her phone for a message. She sighed, unsure if she was disgusted with herself for looking or disappointed there was nothing from the cop hottie.

But there was a new email from Big Jerry at Black Owl. She opened and scanned it, then read the details again. In addition to her regular Tuesday show, he wanted her to add a second one *"on Friday nights for all those lonely souls at home alone on date night."*

She sat back, mulling it over. Big Jerry was assuming she, too, was one of those home alone on date night. That he was correct stung a little, but she brushed the feeling away.

Two shows meant an increased workload, but also more income. Big Jerry had more sponsors interested than he could fit into her 60-minute slot. Since the basic foundation was already established, it wouldn't be twice the effort. She had a growing list of indie bands asking her to feature their music; too many to squeeze in. Sage in Winter, an alternative band out of Toronto, wanted Skyy to debut their upcoming second album. That was two shows right there, especially if she interviewed Sage over Skype.

She typed a reply to Big Jerry that she'd do it, starting the following Friday if that worked for him. His reply was almost instant.

> *Hate to ask, but can you start this week instead of next? I have this Friday open with nothing to fill it.*

Friday was tomorrow. "Here we go," she said, and typed her approval.

Jerry sent a thumbs-up icon, then:

And I need you to change your login to Black Owl again. Added some new security software.

This was the third time in a month. Were others like Creeper breaking through? She had to ask.

Something wrong?

His reply came in several minutes later.

Just taking precautions.

Unease crept up Skyy's neck, but she knew it was probably nothing. With all the data breaches at companies these days, Jerry was wise to take a proactive approach to security, but what a pain for all those who had to change their logins. Although most listeners used a guest access to post messages, thousands created profiles on the Black Owl server to make posting easier. It also allowed them to set up notifications for other shows and events besides *Night Thoughts*.

Skyy logged into Black Owl and changed her credentials. Stalking was never far from her mind, which was exactly why she kept her identity locked down.

With Canon Truax, she was stepping across her own hard line. She prayed it wasn't a huge mistake.

Ember's shift began at 1:00 and lasted thirty-six hours—at least that's how long it seemed. BCJ, short for Backpacking, Coffee, and Jeans, was the first store in what the owners planned to be a nationwide chain. So far it seemed to be working.

She rolled a cart of blue jeans past teens and twenty-somethings lining the coffee bar and overflowing to the bistro tables scattered throughout the store. The idea was to draw them in with the social java vibe and pumping music, then get them seated next to enticing displays of hiking equipment and clothing. REI meets Starbucks. Unlike most other stores that prohibited food and drinks, the owners didn't panic if an occasional spill stained some merchandise.

Nearly every day, the head barista stopped the music and toasted someone's birthday or other special occasion, or offered samples of a new food item or drink. The customers appreciated the freewheeling, friendly atmosphere, and Ember recognized many regulars. How many clothing stores could boast that?

It wasn't a bad place to work, but refolding clothing discarded in the dressing rooms was getting old. Before working here, she never realized people were such slobs and had so little respect for other people's property.

Elliot, the store manager, caught her eye from across the store. He pointed to his watch and jerked his head toward the restrooms. *"Every two hours, rain or shine,"* Elliot repeated at the beginning of every shift. As if the statement made any sense at all for a store inside a mall.

She sighed and headed to fetch the janitorial cart. Three more cleanings before her shift ended. How sad was it she measured her work time by the number of sinks and toilets left to scrub?

On her knees sloshing cleaner around a toilet bowl, she

thought of the lake pictures on Skyy's computer. Beautiful, serene, inspiring. What would it be like to wake up to that every day, to work in a mountain community with fresh, clean air bright with potential?

She flushed the toilet, watching the blue bowl cleaner swirl down and *glug-glug-glug* at the bottom. The sound was beginning to haunt her dreams. She sat back on her heels and wiped her forehead with the back of her wrist.

During her shift, she'd been thinking of Skyy, the lake, and the cop. Skyy would deny it all day long, but her eyes softened when she looked at Cop Hottie's pic. To Ember's admittedly limited knowledge, this was the first time Skyy had shown interest in someone since Loser Boyfriend. Skyy Delaney was a good person and deserved to be happy, and Ember determined to do everything possible to make that happen.

"Almost through in here, Ember?" Elliot asked, rapping his knuckles on the open stall door.

"Two more to go," she said, looking up at him. "You want to finish them for me?"

Elliot laughed. "That's why I hired *you*. Good training for life."

Maybe so. *Life is stinky and full of crap. Get used to it.* True so far.

"Also, one of our valued customers just made a mess of the women's T-shirt display table," Elliot said.

Her next exciting project. He smiled at Ember as he left. Or was it a smirk?

Before moving to the next stall, she spritzed some pine air freshener in the bowl, sure it smelled nothing like the real thing at Cop Hottie's lake.

Ember needed to convince Skyy to search for Canon Truax —and take her along.

CHAPTER 4

"COME ON, TRUAX, GET THAT LAST ONE UP HERE. YOU'RE wasting my time."

Canon wiped the sweat off his brow with his sleeve and stared up at his commanding officer on the road thirty feet above. The bundle of marijuana on his shoulder weighed over twenty pounds. Not that much, but it was bulky and this was his fourth trip up the gully's steep fifty-foot slope of loose rock.

"You want it faster, Cap? How about you throw down a line and pull it up yourself? Then you can spend the rest of the day cooling it at Starbucks."

Captain Tom Olenski laughed and walked away from the edge, leaving Canon to the grunt work. After all, he was the new guy. Even though he wasn't a rookie, he was on loan and new to the unit. Part of his *cross-department training,* his Los Angeles Police Department boss said.

He dug his boots into the shifting rock and continued his struggle. This wasn't the training he imagined.

A homeowner living in a sparsely populated area close to Portrero, California, less than a mile from the Mexican border, reported the four bundles of marijuana. Loud thuds during the night brought the lady out at dawn with her two Dobermans and a Smith & Wesson .357 magnum.

The most likely scenario was the packages detached prematurely from an ultralight aircraft flown across the border. The crafts were known to carry up to ten of the bales strapped to the undercarriage. The routine was to drop them in a predetermined area for pickup by ground contacts. GPS tracking chips made finding the drugs in the dark ridiculously simple. No lights required.

Canon reached the top, weighed the marijuana on a portable scale, then tossed it into the back of their SUV with the others. They were worth about $40,000 on the street, and somebody would be in big trouble over the loss. That made him happy.

He removed his sweat-stained uniform shirt, wetted a towel with water from their Igloo cooler, and wiped his head and neck. According to meteorologists, the whole Southwest was experiencing significantly higher than normal temperatures. He glanced up at the noon sun, convinced.

If nothing came up later today, he was heading for the lake this evening for his three days off. With luck, he'd be there before midnight. The forecast low for tonight was 35 degrees. It sounded perfect.

While Olenski radioed in the tally of their find, Canon checked his phone. It was barely a year old, but the glass had cracked on one corner, and the foggy lower half didn't clear when he wiped it on his pants. As his previous partner liked to say, police work was murder on phones. He spotted the message from Skyy D and tapped it. Two words.

Hi. - ***Skyy***

"Well, I'll be," he said, wishing there were more, but grinning that it was there at all.

"You get some good news, Truax?" the captain said, replacing the mic in its holder.

That remained to be seen. But he was hopeful.

It was nearly 2:00 a.m. when Skyy finished her second shower of the day and dried off. The sheets were calling, but she leaned over to read the message that lit up her phone on the sink counter. She had set up the app to alert her if she received a Black Owl message from select people.

Picked up 85 lbs of marijuana this morning. Good day. - ***Canon***

She shook her head at his choice of response to her first contact. Sounded typical for a cop. Most were stoic and super serious. Okay, other than one local cop here and a state trooper in Nebraska—who both issued her speeding tickets—she hadn't personally met that many. But her impression was that law enforcement types were all in perpetual bad moods.

Did Canon Truax have a sense of humor? He *had* mentioned taking her fishing.

Hmm. That could be a topic for Friday's show. She typed into her notes app: *Do you know any cops with a sense of humor?* The question pressed whether she should respond right away or wait a few hours. Her fingers decided on their own.

Hope you're not keeping it all for yourself. - ***Skyy***

After she sent it, she realized it sounded like she hoped he would share with her. That was the furthest thing from her mind. Her opposition to drugs was a frequent message on her shows, and listeners were quick to argue that pot was harmless. But she'd seen the destruction and tragedy firsthand with her parents and her brother. Living through that had not been fun. Time to revisit the topic.

Drug bust down by the border. Hot nasty business. Took a few hours to get up to the lake where it's near freezing tonight. Would have sent earlier, but no texting or messaging while driving. :-). Hitting the sack. - ***Canon***

GNight. - ***Skyy***

He was at the lake. Freezing. It sounded so good. She flapped her towel to dispel the humid air in the cubicle bathroom. Even though middle of the night, it was still in the upper 70s outside. She hung up the towel, convinced all those people who piously said, *"...but it's a dry heat..."* were completely delusional.

After pulling on sleep shorts and a sleeveless top, she opened her MacBook. She set Google Earth to outline bodies of water, then scanned for lakes "a few hours" from California's southern border.

What did he mean by *few*? Four? Eight? There were zillions of possibilities. Well not that many, but it was still daunting when you added all the reservoirs. Big Bear Lake and Lake Arrowhead might be far enough away, especially with traffic around L.A. She wished she had a clue where Canon had grown up.

The only piece of advice Skyy remembered from her mother popped into her head.

"Never chase a man."

Skyy came home from school one day and said she liked a boy in her sixth-grade class. Mom, slumped on the sofa in a hazy high, had mumbled those words. Two weeks later, their family imploded. Skyy and her brother were whisked away to an aunt and uncle they'd met only once.

What if that boy in sixth grade had been *The One*? She'd thought of him often, a vague outline of a skinny, dark-haired guy. That was all—even his name lost in the on-off mayhem that became her next seven years. Skyy opened her notes application and added more to the one she'd started on the phone.

Have you ever regretted not pursuing someone who might have been The One? How do you know if someone is *The One? Is there* more *than one? Like ten or twenty?*

She stared at the letters on the screen, fingers hovering as she waited for more thoughts to flow. Was that enough? Often a simple question would fill the show, especially if she promoted it a day or two ahead of time. Two shows a week gave her more opportunities to do that.

Finally, she let her hands fall to her lap, realizing further questions were her own, and probably too personal to share. If she was being honest, one thing had changed for her in the last several weeks: when she thought about *The One,* she no longer pictured the boy in sixth grade.

Google Earth and its outlined bodies of water stared back.

You could just ask him.

Yeah, right. Like he would tell her.

She rose from the table and went to dry her hair.

CHAPTER 5

CANON WOKE AT SEVEN O'CLOCK ON FRIDAY MORNING, remaining under the warm covers while he breathed in the cabin's woodsy scent. Although he concentrated, he couldn't quite hear the lake lapping at the shore, but it was there, familiar and waiting, as it had been throughout his childhood.

Even though he'd built a small fire using the remaining pieces of wood last night, the bedroom air wasn't much warmer than it had been when he arrived. And with the ancient forced air furnace dead, it was lucky the water pipes hadn't frozen.

He swung his feet onto the cold rug and rubbed his face. The six-hour drive after the long workday had been mind-numbing. Summer traffic would be even worse, especially if he was still working in San Diego.

After downing some cereal and strong coffee, he headed outside to split the wood Merle Ferris had dumped yesterday by the garage. Merle operated a wide range of business ventures from his location on Old Mill Road in Deer Cove, everything from road grading, to trenching, to tree trimming and firewood.

The cabin's wood stove was a small unit, and most commercially provided wood—including Merle's—was a tight fit through the firebox door. Some wouldn't fit at all. Hand splitting was the cure, and it was a task Canon enjoyed.

His breath came in clouds as he made his way to the shed for the ax and splitter, the air thick and moist under the leaden sky. Rain was coming, and he needed to get the wood under cover.

He stood one of the larger logs on a flat stump and swung the axe. The blade neatly halved the log into two more manageable pieces. He tossed those into a wheelbarrow, then repeated the process.

Noon came and went before he finished stacking the last pieces under the lean-to shelter next to the cabin's carport. He carried three armfuls inside the cabin as the first drops began falling.

After a quick shower, he drove to town in search of food.

Dad and Mom had found the cabin on the north end of Storm Lake nearly forty years ago, one of now twenty houses in an area called Box—named after the rectangular slab of rock rising thirty feet at the shoreline.

Multiple washouts and minor landslides had rendered the road around the top of the lake impassable except by a few hardy souls in four-wheel-drive clubs. This ensured little through traffic by the cabin and spectacular peace and quiet. There were rumors of an effort to reopen it as an alternate escape route, critical if a fire ever swept through the area, but so far nothing had happened.

To the contrary, Deer Cove was anything but quiet. Even in the off-season, a line out the door of Peg's Waffle House wasn't unusual, but it surprised Canon to see several people huddling under umbrellas at four in the afternoon. Hot maple syrup and waffles appeared to be today's popular choice.

Too hungry to wait, he shifted his destination a few doors down. The Crab Shack, a ramshackle gray-sided building with red-framed rear windows, overlooked the marina and lake.

Inside was a buzz of voices and clattering dishes. He breathed in the heavy atmosphere of all things fishy and fried. Framed sales flyers for boats and outboard motors from decades past nestled between fishing poles, nets, floats, wicker creels, and gaff hooks. The front half of a rowboat extended from one wall, repurposed to hold a small salad bar for the health conscious. A teenage girl led him to a table close to a window where a busboy was laying out paper placemats. "This okay?"

"Perfect." Canon sat for a minute, watching the moored sailboats through the glass, which was steamy on the inside and streaked on the outside. Tall masts parried in a perpetual sword fight on the choppy water. Even the protected cove couldn't buffer them from the storm.

"Hey, Canon. The usual?" Molly, a waitress about his age, was already scribbling his order on her pad. She'd worked here for a few years and had a bouncy personality that endured through her long shifts.

"You know me too well, Molly. I'm going to trip you up one of these days."

"Anytime, honey." She winked at him and whirled away toward the kitchen, her blond ringlets flying in a springy halo.

How many times had he come here over the years with his dad, mom, and brother? Each table's scratched surface was unique, and all were familiar to him. Surely the building had once been new, but Canon's earliest memory of it was worn down, slightly seedy, and utterly delicious. Every visit left him full and happy. As comfortable as home.

And it *was* home to some. Canon spotted Merle Ferris sitting at the long bar beside another man with a familiar face. Besides firewood deliveries, Dad hired Merle fifteen years ago to gravel and grade the cabin's driveway. There were other locals Canon recognized among a smattering of winter tourists.

Although he grabbed food alone many times, this time he wished he could share it with someone—and it wasn't his brother who came to mind.

Molly interrupted his thoughts, arriving with a heaping platter of fries, golden-battered fish, tartar sauce, and chilled coleslaw. Before dousing the fries with ketchup, he pulled out his phone and snapped a picture.

Best on Earth! My treat when you join me. - ***Canon***

It was bold saying *when* not *if*, but…well, she hadn't cut him off at the knees yet.

He attached the photo and clicked Send. Most storms wreaked havoc with the cell coverage at the lake. Today he had only one bar of signal, and the progress bar crawled slowly because of the large picture file. He held his breath as it stalled a few times before the message went through.

Satisfied, he picked up the ketchup, gave the fries a liberal dose, and dug in. As always, the food was amazing, but it would be better sharing it with someone.

He was looking forward to Skyy's show tonight.

"Hi, all. Skyy D here, and you're listening to *Night Thoughts* on Black Owl Radio. Hope you're having a good one. And welcome to my first Friday night show in addition to the regular Tuesday gig. Spread the word that we're now on twice each week.

"I'm here for an hour, so please send in some comments and questions on the *Night Thoughts* page. You can also call Black Owl Radio, and they will patch you through to me. And if you have a song or band request, let me know." She recited the phone number and repeated it.

"My topic tonight is a little unusual: Do cops have a sense of humor?"

She told of her two experiences getting speeding tickets, then read a handful of scrolling comments.

"Angelhairblue says, 'My brother is a cop, and he's as funny as a virus.' And this from 2ferrets: 'My boyfriend is a cop. Sweet and funny.'"

Skyy skipped two with punctuation so horrendous she couldn't decipher their meaning. Another dropped f-bombs six times in three sentences. That one rolled down unread. Within a few minutes, the topic morphed into whether cops were generally good guys and gals. Several comments were negative, and Skyy felt the show spinning out of control. Then a window popped to the front on her laptop—a live caller on the line patched in from Big Jerry.

"Is this Skyy D?" The voice was female, young, tentative. Or maybe wary.

"It is. Who am I talking to?" Skyy said into her mic. Big Jerry was doing his tech magic, putting two people in different areas of the country, or even the world, together on her show.

"Uh…I'd rather not say. I mean, if that's okay. Or you can call me K."

"Sure, K is fine." Skyy sat up straighter. Was this the same

K who left the comments? Skyy knew about keeping identities secret, or at least anonymous. She sipped some warm lemon water to keep her throat clear. "Did you have a comment, K?"

"Uh…I had a cop help me once when I was fifteen and on the streets, you know?" She paused for a few seconds. "He was nice. Bought me a hamburger. He didn't want anything. Just to help."

Skyy rubbed her forehead. Fifteen? That voice… What was she, all of sixteen now? "Did he help you find a safe place, K?"

"After I finished my food, I told him I needed to use the bathroom. I slipped out the back door. My, uh…my friend would have been real mad if he knew about the cop, you know?"

"K—"

"I should have—" Tires skidded on pavement in the background. "Gotta go." A dial tone sounded for a few seconds before Big Jerry muted the line.

The girl had hung up.

Shaken, Skyy played some new music to give herself time to process the phone call. Then she cited a university study that said humor improves how people feel about any job no matter how unlikeable it might be. But she was going through the motions, reading scripts and clicking buttons until the show ended. She hoped it didn't sound as flat to the listeners as it did to her.

Every word and syllable of K's young voice was etched in her mind. Was she safe? Had the girl's pimp showed up? There was little doubt that was the *"friend"* K had been talking about. Come next Tuesday or Friday, would she call back? It was moments like these that made the virtual world so frustrating.

"Please call back, K," Skyy said after signing off. "Please." She wanted to help, to finish what the hamburger-buying cop had started.

CHAPTER 6

The weather never improved, so Canon spent the weekend doing maintenance on the four-wheel ATV, raking blown-in debris out of the carport and cleaning the cabin. Smelly, baked-on grease greeted him when he opened the oven.

After spraying cleaner on the mess , he went outside to check the propane tank on the grill. Empty, of course. Mart had been the last one here. He disconnected the tank and set it aside to take into town for a refill, then sent a text to his brother.

CANON:

Next time here, get off ur lazy butt, fill the propane, and cook ur steaks outside. The oven's a mess. Better yet, buy a spare tank and bring it down. Full.

MART:

I'm broke, man. I'll clean the oven next trip.

CANON:

Too late. U owe me.

MART:

5 bucks cover it?

CANON:

Go pose for a calendar photo shoot. Isn't that what u guys do?

MART:

Jealous?

He included a string of rude emojis, making Canon smile.

He hadn't let up on Mart since the Salinas Chamber of Commerce proposed the *Hot Hunks* calendar as a fundraiser. Mart featured prominently as Mr. December, complete with Santa Hat and apparently nothing else thanks to a strategically placed reindeer covering his midsection. Canon's first question was where they'd found a reindeer in California's central valley. Furry animal notwithstanding, he knew Mart had shorts on for the shoot, because if he'd been nude, ten of his buddies would have been snapping pics from behind and blackmailing him.

The calendar project was so successful, there was talk of a new one called *Fiery Fighters*, the name chosen from dozens proposed. Most of the unchosen ones were too risqué to use.

After the final wipe down of the oven, Canon dusted and vacuumed every room. Mart wasn't much for housekeeping, and honestly Canon wasn't much better. Usually.

But all day he'd had the strangest feeling something was going to happen, that he needed to be prepared. How dusting lamps and tables helped, he had no idea.

Maybe it was the *Night Thoughts* phone call on Friday. Canon had been laughing at some of Skyy's comments about cops, when all of a sudden the girl called. Talk about a showstopper. He'd held his breath as Skyy asked K about her experience with cops, and he wondered if Skyy noticed how young the girl sounded. He'd seen more than his fair share of girls on the streets in both L.A. and San Diego. It was a rough life, and they didn't stay young for long. He hoped K would get help before it was too late.

CHAPTER 7

POUNDING WOKE SKYY FROM THE DEAD TUESDAY MORNING AND continued while she stumbled around for something to cover her shorts and T-shirt.

"Coming!" She'd worked until after 1:30 last night processing a flurry of orders for new emoji dolls that were blowing up in her online toy store. She and her competitors were fighting for the few suppliers.

The knocking continued while she rubbed her eyes and considered the clock on the kitchen counter: 7:34 a.m.

She opened the door, recoiling from the blinding sun and squinting at the man standing on the two-by-three foot concrete pad.

"Troy?" Her landlord was dressed for work—Khakis and a black polo with his employer's heavy equipment logo. He fidgeted with his car keys.

"Sorry to disturb you so early, Skyy," he said, his gaze flicking between her and his rubber-soled shoes.

"It's okay." It wasn't, really. With her show later tonight, it was going to be a very long day.

The sun scorched the skin cells on her bare legs while she

waited for him to continue. Taciturn as he was, she couldn't imagine how he made a living as an equipment salesman, but maybe that trait appealed to men and women who used such equipment.

"I've, uh, got some news," he said. More key jiggling. "My daughter and her baby are moving home. Nasty divorce."

"Oh, I'm so sorry, Troy." She knew he was divorced, but not much else. He'd never mentioned children.

"I'm going to need the guest house for them."

"Oh." She stepped back and looked around the tiny room, as if the act could provide more understanding. He was telling her she had to move. She rubbed her eyes, a respite from the outdoor brilliance as she willed herself awake. "When are you thinking?"

He focused on the dead plant in the pot on the step. "They're coming Friday."

"Fri— *This* Friday?" He couldn't seriously be asking her to move in three days.

"I know it's short notice."

"It's *no* notice, Troy." While packing up was not a huge problem, finding a new location most certainly was.

"I'll refund your full deposit," he offered.

She almost laughed. He'd better. But the cash would go fast if she rented motel rooms. And finding a new place to live on three-day's notice would be impossible.

She looked past him to his side yard where a homemade teardrop trailer sat among a half dozen scraggly weeds. Spiderwebs laced the wheel wells, and red dust rose a half inch where it had settled along the bottom sill of each window. But the trailer's aluminum skin shined valiantly under the desert grunge. She'd been looking at it for a while, and felt a kindred spirit in the lonely camper.

"I've got a proposition for you, Troy."

"Hi, all. Skyy D here, and you're listening to *Night Thoughts* on Black Owl Radio. Hope you're having a good Tuesday evening.

"Hey, I've got a question for you. If you could live anywhere in the U.S., where would you go? Maybe you'd like to be on a beach watching the sunrise or sunset, or in a high-rise in Miami, or a Montana mountain, or by a lake. One study says career, family, friends, and climate are the big deciders, but I want to know what *you* say. What's important to you for a place to live?

"While you're thinking about that, here's a pair of songs off the *Kelp EP* by the Flying Whales."

Skyy monitored the scrolling comments, while listening as Big Jerry faded the first song into the second. As prep for the new show starting on Friday, he volunteered to handle more of the technical production, including checking the music links. Skyy arranged the order of songs on the site, which she could change on the fly during a show. A checkbox for each song signaled him to begin play.

A small popup window on her laptop screen showed statistics: number of listeners logged in, waiting phone calls with caller name and Area Code, and show time remaining. Another notes window was available for her to select and drag comments out of the rolling feeds and drop them in so she wouldn't lose them on the scroll.

Skyy tensed when one from Creeper rolled up, but the comment disappeared before she could read it. Big Jerry's controls were working, if not an actual block. She stretched the tension out of her neck, but it wasn't enough to fully dislodge the slimy residue.

Two phone calls were in the queue—a good sign of interest. Skyy was ready with twenty comments by the time the last song faded.

"All right. Some great comments coming in, as well as phone calls. Barryterry6 says definitely by a lake stocked with big trout. Several people say living by water is a must. Pinkjail and four others vote for New York overlooking Central Park. I guess if you're living in NYC, that's not a bad place to land. Others mentioned anywhere with great clubs and theaters. And 95fun&sun says, *'I want water lapping at the shore and mountains that reach for the sky.'*

"And now let's take a call." She clicked the first caller link named Izzy. "Hi, is this Izzy? You're on the air with Skyy D."

"Hi, Skyy! I listen to every show!" The voice was female, bubbly, and Skyy guessed her mid-teens, maybe younger.

"Thanks, Izzy. Have you got a favorite place you'd like to live?"

"I saw this picture of a yacht once that belonged to some rich guy in Southern California. If I lived on a boat like that, I could sail to a new location whenever I wanted."

"Great idea. Where would you pick first?"

"New Orleans…for Mardi Gras!" Someone in the background slurred *"Yeah, baby!"*

Skyy doubted the girl was old enough to drink, but it sounded like the other person had had a few. "Okay, Izzy, I hope you get your yacht someday. Thanks for calling in."

Big Jerry ran a commercial for an organic acne cream, then segued into the next song in the queue, an older number by Pancake Sunset, a group of indie guys out of Philly with incredible talent.

Ember tiptoed through the front door while Skyy was sliding comments over to her notes app.

"It's okay," Skyy said when Ember drew her fingers across her lips in a zipping motion, "there's a song playing right now." She increased the volume on her laptop, making it just loud enough so Ember could hear.

"Ooh, Pancake Sunset," Ember said, setting her backpack on the floor and taking the other chair at the table. "I love their music."

"How do you...?" Skyy shook her head. Ninety-nine percent of the U.S. had never heard of the group, but this girl knew them? She pointed to the clock displaying 12:24 a.m. "What are you doing here? It's way past your curfew."

"You texted me."

"That was like fifteen hours ago."

Ember shrugged. "I was busy."

"Ever heard of calling?"

Ember pointed to the computer. "Song's over."

Skyy saw the counter. The song ended four seconds ago. "Crap."

"Language," Ember said, flashing a cheeky grin as Skyy clicked the mic button.

"We've got some good comments coming in about where you'd live if you could go anywhere in the U.S. Keep them coming." She scrolled through her notes. "Bobby in Brooklyn wants a cabin in the Rockies near the ski slopes. C-EllieRun picks Phoenix because she likes the heat."

Skyy shuddered at that one, and Ember slapped a hand over her mouth, her body shaking silently. Skyy shot her a look and pointed at the hot mic as a reminder.

"Dozens of people want homes right on the beach," Skyy said. "Malibu, Galveston, Cape Cod, Maui and all places Hawaii. San Diego has the most votes, though.

"ConnieC3 wants family nearby, and Albertmarkedassafe in Oklahoma City says being with the one you love is more important than location. Aww, isn't that romantic? Too bad we're past Valentine's Day." A flurry of heart emoji comments followed—probably by those teen girls.

Skyy laughed. "Well, it sounds like Albertmarkedassafe has won the ladies' hearts tonight. And *no*, girls, I can't give out his contact information. Sorry.

"Here's some new music by Jen & Harley from Akron, called 'Inappropriate Ingredients.' I hope it's not a love song, but tell me what *you* think. And after this, I'll take the next caller, so hang in there, CT." She muted her mic.

"You're pretty good at this," Ember said, rising and opening the refrigerator.

"I've had lots of practice."

Ember came back with an Orange Crush. "I could do it."

"You vying for my job?" Skyy kept her tone light, but she was quite cognizant that, at twenty-nine years old, she could lose relevancy for the younger generation. While her knowledge, life questions, and feelings were maturing, her listeners were regularly replaced by the next crop of upcoming teens and young adults. Sure, she had some listeners in their forties, fifties, and even older, but the demographic surveys Big Jerry ran consistently showed the bulk of her audience fell into the 16 to 30 range. The key was working to stay in touch with those fans, delve into issues they confronted in this changing world.

"Nah," Ember said. "I'm just saying, if you ever need a fill-in, I'm your girl. I've got topic ideas enough for a year."

Skyy watched Ember lift the can to her lips. This was a special girl with mountains of potential—if life would only give her a break. But Skyy wouldn't get to see that happen. She was moving in three days.

"I need to tell you something," Skyy said.

"How did you get your name?" Ember asked. "With the two Ys, I mean."

Skyy scrunched her brow at the right turn in subject, but it gave her a reprieve from confessing her move. "It was from my father. His favorite brand of vodka."

Ember laughed. "Good thing he didn't like Grey Goose."

Skyy smiled. That's exactly what she thought when she discovered the link between her name and alcohol. Although she considered changing it, by the time she found out the truth, she had settled into the name. That she consciously chose to keep it made the decision hers, not her parents'.

"I heard you're moving," Ember said, her own smile slipping. Her tone was buoyant, hopeful, but fear showed in the tight lines around her mouth.

Skyy shouldn't be surprised the girl knew. "Troy came by this morning. That's why I sent the text." She explained about his daughter and granddaughter moving in.

Ember rubbed her fingers up and down the side of the soda, staring at the evaporating condensation. "I was serious the other day when I said I want to go with you."

"I know," Skyy sighed, noting on the monitor the current song would run out in fifteen seconds. It wasn't enough time to dive into this discussion, and Ember needed to get home. "Can you come by tomorrow after school so we can talk more?"

Ember sat still for long seconds, then nodded as the song ended.

Relieved, Skyy keyed the mic button and leaned close. "And now will take that next caller. Hi, CT, this is Skyy D. Thanks for holding. Tell me, where would you like to live?"

"Hi, Skyy. Let's see..." His voice was deep, mellow, like he'd woken from a nap. Not a teenager. "Well, I sort of already have a place I like, but I don't get to live there full time."

"Tell me about it," Skyy said, leaning back in her chair. She closed her eyes, letting his voice fill her headphones.

"My parents died and left a cabin to my brother and me. It's on a lake in California."

Skyy straightened and cut a glance at Ember who was still playing with the moisture on her soda can.

"Our cabin is old and needs some work, but it has a great view down the length of the lake. The weather is cold right now, and I have a fire going in the wood stove. Summers are when everything comes alive. Lots of kids swimming, people boating, tubing, barbecuing hot dogs at the swimming beach. And the ocean's not far."

Ember snapped up, wide eyes locked on Skyy.

"I guess the thing I like most is that people who live here know each other. When I go to town, they call me by name."

"It sounds wonderful, CT," she said. She had to take a drink of lemon water to clear the growing lump in her throat. Truth was, it *did* sound wonderful. A real life mash-up of the iconic *Cheers* bar and the town of *Mayberry RFD*. But those were television fiction—*old* fiction from simpler times. Could such places exist in the real world?

"My job down south is pretty stressful, so I take every opportunity to get here, kick back, get dirty, and go jump in the lake." He laughed. "When it's not freezing, that is."

"Is it far from where you live and work?"

"I wrangled an extra day off, but I have to leave early tomorrow to go back. It's a few hours' drive."

Despite the nighttime heat pressing through her shed's thin walls, goose bumps rose on her arms.

"That's a long way," she said, her voice came out wispy, but she resisted the urge to clear it.

"It's worth it. The worst thing is, I can't text and drive."

Ember bounced in her chair and mouthed, *It's him!*

Skyy realized she was grinning too.

When CT, aka Canon Truax, hung up, it was Ember who remembered to click the checkbox for Big Jerry to play the next song.

CHAPTER 8

Skyy held her breath while the Arizona Motor Vehicles Department inspector peered at each trailer light, checking boxes on a clipboard form as she went.

Troy promised the electrical wiring was in good condition. He had been reluctant to trade her the trailer instead of returning her rent deposit, which hadn't been a lot of money, but she played the guilt card. He was basically kicking her to the curb with barely any notice. Plus, she knew he bought it for a song, intending to restore it and take it camping. He'd done neither.

Ultimately, he even agreed to pay the neighbor boy to wash the trailer, Armor All the tires, and vacuum every square inch of the bare plywood interior. The little fenders were painted a red close enough to the finish of her fifteen-year-old Jeep Cherokee, that the clerk said it looked like a matched set.

"Okay, hon," the woman said, scrawling her signature on the clipboard. "Might want to get those tires replaced before you tow it too far. Got some sidewall cracking. Other than that, looks like you're good to go."

Skyy breathed a sigh of relief and left the office a few

minutes later with a new title and registration sticker. The little teardrop was hers.

The trailer's lift-up rear hatch contained an outdoor kitchen compartment, consisting solely of a tiny sink with a faucet fed by pump from a five-gallon tank mounted under the cabinet. That was it.

At her favorite thrift store, she scored a single burner propane stove for seven bucks, a $3.00 ice chest that, from the black scuff marks, looked like it had skidded down a roadway, and a pint-sized microwave in its original box for $8.00. The used sleeping bags that who-knew-what had slept in—or what was still living inside—didn't even tempt her. A girl had to draw the line somewhere. She swung by Target for a new bag and an air mattress.

The store parking lot had several pull-through spaces, making it easy to park the Jeep and trailer. But Skyy worried all the way home about how she could back the trailer into the driveway. Fortunately, Troy's house was on a quiet street, so she drove just past the driveway and cranked the steering wheel first one way, then the other, trying to aim the rear of the trailer into the narrow entrance.

Her frustrating efforts were made all the worse by the teen neighbor boy watching her from astride his bike on the sidewalk.

"You want me to guide you back?" he asked after her fifth attempt. She pulled forward a couple of feet, snapping off a branch from Troy's hedge. If she kept this up, he wouldn't have to trim the hedge for months. Maybe ever.

"I—"

"I used to pull a trailer," said a woman Skyy recognized as the boy's mother. "I'm Wanda, by the way," she said, offering her hand through the driver window.

"Skyy." She shook the woman's hand. "I'm afraid this is

my first time. Never thought backing up would be so challenging."

"It's tricky," Wanda nodded, "especially with a short trailer like this. But here's the key: put both hands on the bottom of your steering wheel."

Skyy did as instructed.

"Now, whichever direction you move your hands, that's the way the back end of the trailer will swing. That's all you have to remember."

Wanda pulled her boy to safety as Skyy processed the instructions and tried again. *"That's all..."* may have been an oversimplification. It took her a several more times to maneuver the trailer down the side driveway until it was near her guest house. She turned off the car and got out. Three good-sized hedge branches and a dozen smaller ones lay on the dirt.

"Whew. I hope I don't have to do that again." Sweat dripped down the middle of her back, and the sun glaring off the aluminum trailer was like standing next to a solar furnace. She moved into the shade of the house.

"Oh, you'll have it down in no time," Wanda said. "I've been watching this little trailer wasting away over here for years. Glad to see it's getting some use. Are you taking it camping? I've got plenty of equipment if you need to borrow anything."

Skyy shook her head. "Actually, I'm moving on Friday. I'm staying in the trailer as I travel."

"Oh," Wanda said, her voice sagging. "Well then, I feel bad about not introducing myself sooner."

Not for the first time, Skyy wondered if there was something wrong with her ability to connect with others. She rarely got to know neighbors. Wanda seemed a caring, warm person, and she'd been right next door the whole time Skyy lived in Tucson. It could be because each place she moved felt temporary, like a motel room—not a place to establish friendships and roots. Or was it a deeper wariness of relationship, ground into her after Loser Boyfriend's sudden departure?

The virtual world was far safer. That's where her business was—and, perhaps sadly, almost all her relationships. A hurtful comment or obnoxious person could be banished with a click. No confrontation, little stress, gone forever. But in real life, broken trust and betrayal ran deep, leaving torn edges that resisted healing—at least not without an ugly scar.

"Where are you moving to?"

"What?" Skyy blinked away the troubling thoughts and focused on the woman standing next to her.

"Sorry, I didn't mean to be nosy," Wanda said. "You don't have to answer. But I've always loved it here in Tucson. Perfect place to live, far as I'm concerned. I was just curious where you were going? Someplace special to you?"

Skyy turned to her Cherokee and trailer, imagining them loaded with her few possessions, rolling down the road. But there were no signs along the way telling her where the road led. How could she pull out of the driveway and not know which direction to go? She turned back to Wanda.

"I have no idea."

Wanda appeared nonplussed, but then forced a smile. "Well, I'm sure it will be great—for you." The woman mumbled her goodbye, then walked down Troy's driveway, skirting the litter of hedge branches.

Skyy rubbed her forehead, knowing she needed to get her act together and make a plan. But the destination that kept rising to the top was Cheers or Mayberry on a lake. Wherever Canon Truax was.

Hours later, Skyy pulled off the bandana tied around her forehead and wrung it out. A small puddle of mud formed in the dirt at her feet, disappearing into the parched earth even as she watched.

"After ten o'clock at night and still cooking," she said to the dark. "That's the Tucson I know and love. *Not*." Leaving couldn't come soon enough.

The back seats of the Jeep were folded down, and the cargo space was already half filled. By the time she loaded the rest of the boxes, it would be up to the headliner in some spots. That could be a good thing, preventing glare in her rearview mirror off the shiny trailer.

She should have filled the passenger seat too, but it was still empty, perhaps evidence of her indecision about Ember going along. The girl hadn't come by after school as promised. Had she changed her mind? That possibility bothered Skyy. And the fact that it did so, bothered her as well.

"I'm too used to being alone," she mumbled. Maybe she should get a dog. It could ride in the passenger seat and bark at passing trucks. At least she'd have someone—some*thing*—alive to talk to.

Wanda had returned at sunset and showed Skyy how to distribute her belongings for good weight balance. Only lighter things went inside the trailer: clothes, dry foods, towels, paper products, and her sleeping gear. Canned food was in a box in the Cherokee, and all but minimal cleaning supplies were remaining behind for Troy's daughter. The bed, cookware, and most of the furniture came with the rental.

The more Wanda talked about fishtailing and using low gears going up and down hills, the more nervous Skyy became. Then the woman piled on instructions for leveling and stabilizing the trailer at a campsite. Fortunately, she demonstrated it all. It was a lot to remember, and Skyy was grateful when Wanda wrote out a simple checklist to follow when hitching and unhitching.

Skyy switched off the porch light and sank to the stone step by her door, waiting for her eyes to adjust to the night. Several weeks ago, she joined a group sponsored by a local planetarium for a trip into the desert. They pulled off the highway and followed a dirt road for a mile or so as it climbed up a low hill. When the car lights went out, a million stars filled the heavens, increasing in multitude by the second as her eyes adjusted. The leaders set up telescopes and passed around binoculars.

Here in town the stars were far fewer, muted by the wash of city light. But she would never forget the splash of the Milky Way, the belt of Orion, W-shaped Cassiopeia, or the Big Dipper's outline. It was one thing she'd miss about the desert.

She wiped her forehead on her shirtsleeve. Stars, yes, but not the heat.

The shower beckoned, but she feared she was too tired to get up. She still had to clean the guest house tomorrow, but that wouldn't take long now that most of the packing was finished. Then she was free to leave whenever she chose. But when she drove out of the driveway, where would she go? In all her moves, she'd never been this unclear about the next step.

"Skyy?" A curse followed the bang of the plastic waste bin beside the main house.

"Over here," Skyy said, clicking on her phone's screen so Ember could make her way across the yard. This was a conversation she didn't want to have but couldn't avoid.

"Did your porch light burn out?" Ember asked.

"Just seems cooler with it off."

Ember laughed and sat down next to Skyy. "I've lived here my whole life. Believe me, darkness doesn't help the heat." They sat side by side in silence for a minute, the diffused city lights revealing a monotone gray.

"I thought you were coming by earlier. Guess you knew I was doing a lot of sweaty stuff."

"I had to go into work and do some things. And I had to talk with Mrs. Oso." She cleared her throat. "So, you're all packed up?"

Skyy nodded, knowing what was coming next. Mrs. Oso ran Ember's group home. If Ember was talking to her…

"I want to go." Ember's voice quivered slightly, but there was determination in her tone.

Skyy pinched the bridge of her nose. "It's not that simple. I don't even know where I'm going."

"It *is* simple," Ember said. "You leave and I go with you. That's it."

"But the transition home is a good place."

"Sure, for two more months. Then it's *sayonara, baby,* and I'll be living in a cardboard box down by the river."

"No you won't. You'll find a roommate, rent a place. There are other resources. And you already have a job."

Ember shot her a look. "Cleaning toilets at BCJ? Do you know how much retail pays?"

Skyy did know. On *Night Thoughts,* she'd talked with both boys and girls who had aged out of their foster systems at eighteen with a minimum pay job. Or worse, no job, no transportation, and no place to live. Some states and counties were better than others in equipping kids for the transition, but most provided the barest resources for young people being on their own at such a young age. And because of their screwed-up home lives, they were less prepared than teens who came from a stable situation.

The smack-in-the-face reality was, if Skyy and her brother's aunt and uncle hadn't taken them in, they might have been in the same position as Ember. In all Skyy's time on her own in her twenties, she'd never been as close to homelessness as Ember was right now. *Two months*. It was unfair to downplay the girl's trepidation.

"I've saved up," Ember said. "I can pay my own way."

"Or," Skyy countered, "I could try to find another place here in town for a while longer, give us some time to decide. I need an Internet connection for my show tomorrow night, but I could probably sneak back here and park on the street." Troy's Wi-Fi router had a strong signal.

"That's what you want to do? Stay in Tucson?"

She sighed. No, it wasn't at all what she wanted. Lupe was gone off to Florida, and now that the packing was a done deal, Skyy was itchy to strike out. Finding another rental in Tucson had zero appeal. Even if she found an RV park near town for a few days to give her and Ember time to work things out, living in the trailer without air conditioning was not an option.

She shook her head, both in answer to Ember's question, and in denial of her own stupid desire. What she wanted was to find a place by a lake. *His* lake.

"I…" Ember's voice was a whisper on the night breeze, tinged now with desperation, pleading. "I'll pay you to take me."

Vance's words from years ago popped into her head. Skyy had been agonizing about deciding a college, endlessly weighing the pros and cons, when her brother said, "*What's the worst that could happen?*" That simple question helped her pick a school. If things didn't work out, she could always change. Choices weren't permanent.

Except it hadn't worked out so well for her brother. Had Vance asked himself that same question before he shot up with heroin the first time?

What's the worst that could happen?

She noticed a small duffel at Ember's feet. "What's in the bag?"

"Half my stuff. I won't take up much room." There was hope in her voice, fortified with determination.

"Your group home…"

"Every few days they talk to us about leaving to make our own way," Ember said. "They'll be glad I'm going early. Frees up space for someone else coming out of foster."

Skyy looked at the girl's profile in the dark. Ember's choice was as uncertain as Skyy's—a murky future on the road in a tin can trailer with a woman she barely knew. But regardless of risk and the complete unknown, Ember had made her decision.

She thought again about the caller, the young girl named K. Other than offering advice of sometimes questionable value, Skyy couldn't directly help people online. But here was a chance to help this young woman get a start in life, to actually make a real difference in her future. And Ember had a mind and will of her own. She wasn't asking Skyy to take care of her, only to allow her to go along.

"You talked to Mrs. Oso about this?"

"Oh, yeah," Ember laughed, relief filling her voice. "She insists on meeting you tomorrow, before noon."

"Should I be worried?" Skyy asked.

"Nah, she's a pussycat."

Right. That wasn't Ember's previous description of the woman.

"Okay," Skyy said. "I'll meet you there at 11:00."

"Thank you!" Ember rose to her knees and threw her arms around Skyy, nearly knocking them both onto the dusty yard. "I won't let you down."

"Easy," Skyy said around the sudden lump in her throat. "You don't have to prove anything to me. We're just two gals on the road. You know, like Thelma and Louise—except without the crime and murder and stuff. And the ending."

Eyes wide, Ember sat back. "Who are Thelma and Louise?"

Skyy waved away the question. Her age was showing. "Old story. Never mind."

"Gotcha," Ember said, laughing and pushing Skyy's shoulder. "I've seen it twice. Mrs. Oso shows it every month as an example of what not to do."

"I think I'm going to like your Mrs. Oso."

Ember laughed at that.

"What?"

"So," Ember said, sobering and ducking the question, "eleven tomorrow morning?"

Skyy nodded. "Then we'll go shopping to get you a sleeping bag, air mattress, and anything else you need."

CHAPTER 9

"Hi, all. Skyy D here, and you're listening to Skyy D at Night on Black Owl Radio, and this is *Night Thoughts*. Hope you're having a good evening. Thanks for dropping in for my ramblings and to hear some great music from independent artists all over the world.

"A word of warning: I'm broadcasting tonight from the parking lot of a coffee shop. Sort of borrowing their Wi-Fi, so don't tell anyone. If I disappear for a while, or permanently, Big Jerry might have to step in."

She clicked the next queued song, signaling Big Jerry to begin the fade-in. "Here's a new one by Rocket Dogs out of Orlando, Florida. Tell me if you like their Latin punk."

"Latin punk?" Ember laughed. She sat in the passenger seat of the Cherokee, balancing the laptop while Skyy held the microphone.

"Takes all kinds," Skyy said. "There are dozens of genres of punk, but I like Rocket Dogs because they're straightforward, good-time club music."

"Great idea. We should go dancing," Ember said, staring out at the dark parking lot. It was as deserted as the rest of the town, and it wouldn't be odd if a rabid coyote skulked around the building's corner. *Club* probably wasn't a term often used in the same sentence as *Gila Bend, Arizona.*

Their travel adventure began derailing this morning when the right-side trailer tire blew 45 minutes past Casa Grande as they drove west on Interstate 8. Ember had lifted a skeptical eyebrow at the spare tire's glossy black, but cracked, sidewalls as they struggled to tighten the lugs. Sure enough, it endured only to the outskirts of Gila Bend before it dramatically self-destructed like its brother. Skyy limped into Harv's Fuel Stop, the tire throwing chunks of rubber all over the weed-sprouted pavement as the steel rim gouged the surface.

Harv himself helpfully pointed out a bulge on the sole surviving tire. Decidedly *un*-helpful was the fact Harv didn't have any of the 14-inch tires in stock, nor a new rim to replace the mangled one sinking deep into the hot blacktop. Naturally, the nearest tire distributor was closed for the night.

Skyy kicked herself for choosing I-8 instead of I-10 where there was more help available, but she'd wanted to avoid the heavier traffic around Phoenix while she got used to towing the trailer. That's what she'd told Ember. The fact that Canon Truax was working near the Mexican border might have influenced her route. I-8 entered California at its southernmost part. Not that she knew where he was. Not yet.

"Earth to Skyy," Ember said, poking Skyy's forearm. "Song's over."

Skyy cleared her throat, pushing away the image of the lawman exiting the surf.

"Hey. Have you ever wondered about choices and how they change your life? For instance, the reason I'm hopping on a coffee shop Wi-Fi is I'm stranded in a small town until tomorrow with two flat tires. If I'd chosen a different route, I might have been in the bigger city with more services. Or, if I hadn't chosen Loser Boyfriend that night at the dance club, I might have found a better guy a few days later.

"Have you made a big choice lately? How do you know if you made the right one? Post your thoughts or call in. Meanwhile, here's "Me Talking to Me," by Ciara Olivera from Austin, Texas."

While Rocket Dogs had been an upbeat opener, Olivera's song sought meaning out of a life of disappointments. The lyrics told of the singer's attempt to encourage herself. Skyy could use some of that right now. She shook off the fatigue that had plagued her all day.

"I thought you were talking about integrity tonight," Ember said, sliding the laptop onto the dash. There was just enough room between the seats to reach the small cooler in back. She popped the top on an orange soda, her fingers fiddling with the can's aluminum ring. "Are you having doubts about me coming along?"

The words were playful, but the way she wouldn't meet Skyy's gaze spoke the real meaning.

This morning while Ember packed her last belongings at the group home, Amelia Oso had cornered Skyy.

"Ember shows a lot of outward bravado, but it's a fragile façade," the woman said.

Mrs. Oso was five feet tall and had the personality of an irritated badger—reinforced by the whitish streak in her black hair. She began frowning as soon as Ember excitedly introduced Skyy and disappeared upstairs.

"She talks about you all the time, Ms. Delaney, but it's a mistake for her to go with you."

When their girl bounced down the stairs with two black

garbage bags and a big smile, Mrs. Oso leaned close to Skyy and growled, *"Do not screw this up."*

Tendrils of desert cool trickled in through the cracked car windows. Not enough to drain away all the day's heat, but it was a start.

Don't screw this up. Skyy touched Ember's arm and waited until their eyes met.

"No doubts, Ember Peyron. I'm glad you're here. You could go anywhere, yet you picked a nearly broke trailer-park woman with bad tires who has no idea where she's going. That's bravery."

Ember laughed, and this time it reached her eyes. She grabbed the laptop off the dash, and Skyy lifted her mic.

"Okay, we're back and talking about choices. Animal-lover in Baltimore says she makes pros and cons columns for bigger decisions. I've tried that a couple of times; it works pretty well. Darktrey and several others ask a family member." Not a luxury available to Skyy. Nor for the girl beside her.

"A study by the Arnnesson Institute in Florida found that 67 percent of college students haven't got a good methodology on making decisions. The majority say *gut feeling* is important, or whatever makes them happy. To me, that sounds sort of egotistical. The older I get, the more knowledge I gain, but making choices isn't necessarily easier. Have you heard the phrase 'You don't know what you don't know'? It means there are some important things to consider that we don't even know exist. That's where outside help is critical.

"But you have to choose that outside help carefully. According to the study, most consult friends. That can be like pooling ignorance. I mean, if you've got a bunch of people with little knowledge or experience, how can they help you with big decisions? Seems like that could get you in a lot of trouble."

That brought in a flurry of responses. Some accused her of being a pessimist, a couple said she should *"listen to the Universe"* with a capital U, whatever that meant. Others suggested rolling dice and *"going for it."*

"I'm putting up a survey on the website," she said. "Vote your favorite P word: parents, psychics, prayer, procrastinate, punt. Meanwhile, here's music from another P, Phidel out of London." She clicked the play button for Big Jerry, and a moody, indie pop number typical of the singer began. Skyy posted the P-word survey on the *Night Thoughts* page of the Black Owl website.

"I'm not sure which one I'd pick." Ember balanced the laptop on the dash again and pointed to the survey. "Do you ever pray?"

Skyy thought about the question. A neighbor had taken her to church a few times when her parents first started sliding toward the dark side. The stories and activities with other kids were fun, but most of all she liked the positive messages of love, acceptance, forgiveness, and second chances. With that kind of emphasis, she wondered why going to church wasn't more popular. Why was it easier to believe in the Universe—capital U and all—than God? Maybe the Universe didn't hold people to better behavior. No guilt if you chose whatever you wanted and royally screwed up.

"Skyy?"

"Oh, sorry." Skyy opened her mouth, and then remembered Amelia Oso's warning: *Don't screw this up.* She picked her words carefully. "I think the correct answer about praying is always '*not as much as I should.*'"

What she was really thinking was, *Delaney, you'd better get your act together if you're going to be an example to this girl.* Prayer might be a good idea.

She glanced at the laptop screen with its scrolling posts, each signed by a real person from somewhere in the world. It was a lot easier to give advice and be an example to people she'd never met.

CHAPTER 10

"FINALLY," EMBER SAID MONDAY MORNING AT 11:45. SHE climbed in the Cherokee and slammed the door. "Let's blow this town before something else goes wrong."

Skyy couldn't agree more. The parts truck delivered the wrong size tires on Saturday, and Skyy and Ember spent Sunday in Phoenix hunting down the correct ones.

She wasn't even surprised this morning when Harv discovered a worn wheel bearing on the trailer. Fortunately, the bearing was carried by the local parts store. Still, it had cost them a couple more hours on top of the three days. The town was like a glue that wouldn't let them go.

As Skyy drove out of Gila Bend, she pictured dollar bills scattering in the trailer's wake like so many leaves, with Harv, the motel owner, and the parts store clerk chasing after them, dancing happily as they snatched up the money.

After forty minutes driving, Skyy shifted in her seat and rolled her shoulders to loosen the knots. She'd been expecting another shoe—or two or three—to drop, for Murphy to show up with his law again. But everything was going smoothly.

"Stop!" Ember yelled.

Skyy stomped the brake pedal, wrestling the steering

wheel as the trailer's weight pushed the Cherokee's rear back and forth. The Jeep tires slid in gravel on the apron of the freeway as she guided the car to a stop.

"What? Did I hit something?" Her heart hammered in her chest, and dust swirled past the windows, engulfing the car in a tan cloud. She checked her side mirror. Traffic was mercifully light, the nearest car a half-mile back. The trailer was still attached and appeared to be level, so it hadn't lost a wheel or tire.

"Look!" Ember said, pointing out the passenger window.

Skyy leaned across the center console to follow the girl's finger, expecting to spot an animal carcass lying in a pile of blood and bones. But Ember was pointing to a billboard fifty feet on the other side of a barbed wire fence.

World Famous Date Shakes. Next Exit.

Ember turned to Skyy, grinning, her eyes bright. "Let's stop and get some." She must have noticed Skyy's expression, for her grin disappeared. "What?"

Skyy shook her head and collapsed back into her seat. A shadow darkened her side window and she jumped. A man dressed in a plaid shirt and jeans stood there for a moment, then motioned to roll down her window. As she lowered it, the side mirror revealed a big rig parked behind them, its emergency flashers pulsing.

"You ladies okay?" he asked, bending down and peering inside. "You were all over the road back there." He had an Arizona Diamondbacks baseball cap on his head.

Skyy couldn't help herself and started laughing. "*I'm* okay. But this one..." she pointed a finger at Ember "...I'm not so sure about."

The man removed his cap and scratched his head.

Perhaps the hot weather caused the long line at the order counter, or maybe it was the shake's popularity, because every vehicle traveling the Interstate seemed to pull into the parking lot.

It certainly wasn't the discount pricing. Skyy checked her thinning wallet. She'd have to find an ATM soon.

The cost of the shakes consumed their entire lunch budget, but when the first taste slid down her tongue, Skyy had to admit, the wait and cost was worth it. "Whoa, that's good."

"I know, right?" Ember's cheeks indented as she sucked the thick mixture through the straw.

Skyy didn't want to know the calorie count, but the sugar content alone had them both in a near coma by the time they climbed back into the Jeep.

"I think I'm too dizzy to drive," Skyy said, resting her head against the steering wheel. "My heart's palpitating. It's as bad as downing a grande margarita on an empty stomach."

"I wouldn't know about that," Ember said, noisily vacuuming the bottom of her foam cup.

"I hope not."

"Want me to drive?"

Skyy rolled her forehead on the steering wheel so she could see the girl. "You have a license?"

"Uh, not technically. But I know how to drive."

"Someone taught you?"

Ember shook her head. "Video games at my last two foster homes. I totally killed everyone on Xbox."

"That's what I'm afraid of."

"Oh, come on. I can *so* do this. You've already had a shake for lunch instead of your usual healthy stuff. Take a risk."

Risk. That's what she'd done in the bar in Minneapolis eight months ago, where she'd gone to search for her brother. Vance had called and left a message asking for money. When she called the number back, a bartender answered the payphone.

She hadn't been an airhead that night. She kept a hand on the drink that the friendly man on the next stool insisted on buying her. At least she thought so.

He was tall, well-shaped from regular workouts, and reasonably handsome. Introduced himself as Eric or Rick or Brick or Brock...or something. They danced to three or four songs—exactly what she needed after a stressful two days hunting for Vance.

He seemed like a nice guy—the man in the bar, not her brother. He coached soccer for his niece's team and ate dinner at his parents' house every Sunday. Yep, a nice guy.

Until things got fuzzy and then disappeared entirely.

Police told her that two women coming out of the restroom surprised the guy half dragging Skyy down the hall toward the rear exit. They called him out. He shoved Skyy toward them, then slammed through the door. She woke up in the E.R. hours later with a ripping headache, a missing handbag, and little memory of what happened.

The description the two women gave police matched a sketch of a guy who was a known offender. Seven women told a similar story. Three more women couldn't tell *their* stories. They were dead.

Risk—and Eric/Rick or whoever—was dangerous. Which was why, as soon as she returned home from Minneapolis, she packed everything and hightailed it out of Biloxi, landing in Tucson with a new Arizona driver's license, a new credit card and, hopefully, no perv following her from Minnesota.

She shivered at what she was doing now. Yeah, Canon Truax *seemed* like a nice guy, but what did she really know? Some guys probably were nice. Some definitely weren't. How did you tell the difference? She couldn't shake the feeling she was taking a risk she shouldn't.

Skyy reluctantly gave up the support of the steering wheel, leaned back in her seat, and opened her *Show Ideas* file on her phone. *How do you know if he's a nice guy?* Then, just to keep all things equal: *Or if she's a nice girl? What questions do you ask? What do you* need *to know?* She could begin with what characteristics were important, then talk about which questions revealed those. No doubt someone would call with a horror story about—

"So…am I driving?"

Skyy shot Ember a glance, then turned the key in the ignition. "After you get your license."

A minute later, she merged the Jeep and little teardrop onto the Interstate. If only dating were as simple as learning to drive.

It took Canon several tries before he struggled to a sitting position on the side of his bed, sweating and groaning from the effort. He picked up his buzzing cell phone from the nightstand.

"Yeah?"

"Happy Monday, bro," Mart said.

He sat breathing heavily, contemplating whether to talk to his brother or toss the phone and make for the bathroom. Mart's chipper tone had the bathroom winning on points.

"Shoulder still bad?" Mart asked when Canon didn't answer.

Friday night, a joint task force raided a warehouse a mile north of the border. He had tackled a wiry Hispanic male and was putting zip ties on his wrists when a dozen men poured in from a room leading to a hidden underground tunnel. Things went south from there, and the ensuing brawl left Canon with bruised ribs and an egg-sized knot on the back of his head. But the worst was the searing pain in his right shoulder.

"Bad doesn't begin to describe it."

The emergency room doc said ice it, and that he'd probably need physical therapy. Captain Olenski hadn't been happy about that at all. He suggested Canon do the ice for a few days and wait and see on the P.T. As soon as Canon arrived at his home in L.A., he crawled into bed with ice packs. But now was day three, and there wasn't enough ice in the world to fix this.

"I've got two days off," Mart said. "Want me to come down?"

He tentatively lifted his right arm across his chest, wincing as pain radiated across his back like a burning electric current. Sweat dotted his forehead as he eased his arm back to its resting position.

"I have a doctor's appointment in an hour. That's if I can get some clothes on. I'll call you with the results."

Five hours and an MRI later, he was on the department's disabled list and scheduled for shoulder surgery Tuesday afternoon.

CHAPTER 11

"YIKES, IT'S FREEZING OUT HERE." EMBER SWUNG HER LEGS OVER the picnic table bench and sat opposite Skyy. The girl had been reading in the Cherokee. It probably wasn't much warmer, but at least the interior wasn't breezy.

"It was so nice yesterday," Skyy said, pulling a blanket tighter around her shoulders. At nearly 4,000 feet elevation, Pine Valley, California had been a blessed reprieve from the heat that dogged them all the way from Gila Bend. The private campground of forty spaces had fewer than a dozen occupants. With no specific destination in mind—and with decent Wi-Fi here—the camp seemed like a good location to spend a couple of days. Skyy could plan out her shows, manage her online stores, and figure out her next move.

Last night was great. They washed a load of clothes in the laundry room, cooked dinner, and showered in the serviceable camp bathroom before the evening grew too cool.

Today was a different story. It was only 3:30, but high clouds began scurrying overhead at noon and were darkening by the minute. The camp proprietor said rain would come before midnight. Leaves swirled around the picnic table legs, propelled by a breeze scented with pine and hints of ozone. Ozone meant lightning. And they were in a metal trailer.

"Who would have thought the temperature could drop so fast?" Ember said as she lit the burner on the camp stove and arranged the folding metal shield as a reflector. It worked slightly better than nothing at all, and they both rubbed their hands in front of the hissing blue flame.

It sounded warmer than the reality. As often as not, the wind blew the heat away before it got to them. Even with the blanket, Skyy's shoulders were shaking.

"How can you even type?" Ember said.

Big Jerry had tonight's show notes and song list, and the laptop screen was dark from inactivity. It wasn't typing or planning the show that had kept her rooted to the frozen boards so long her butt went numb. No, something else triggered a deep unease.

Was it that she hadn't heard from Canon Truax? No comment after his call-in to last Tuesday's show. Wednesday and Thursday passed with nothing. Then Friday's show came and went. Still no contact.

Had she misread the caller? Maybe it wasn't Canon after all. She shook her head. No, it was him. She was sure of it. So was Ember, who encouraged Skyy every hour to check her phone for messages.

But no message came, and she'd been sitting out here hoping he was just busy chasing bad guys. Her nose was running, and she'd spent much of the last hour with her fingers tucked in her armpits. All the while, her internal sensors flared and sputtered about a cop.

Ember pushed the laptop screen closed and slid it aside so she could scoot the camp stove closer between them. "Think we'll be warm enough in the trailer tonight?" A shiver shook her small body.

Skyy sighed. Their combined breathing last night had the metal walls dripping with condensation in no time, and that was with warmer temperatures. Cracking two of the windows helped, but they let in cold air. Tonight, they would indeed freeze—if they weren't struck by lightning.

Ember was looking to Skyy for answers, and not only about staying warm. Unfortunately, Skyy had only lots of questions. Planning for the future had never been a strong suit, and women's intuition about knowing what to do was a myth for her.

The best advice she'd ever gotten from her aunt was *"One step at a time."*

Maybe that was enough for now. One thing for sure, she was tired of freezing. She grabbed Ember's hands and rubbed them with her own.

"Okay, here's the plan: we drive to the store and buy an electric heater, a pizza, and one of those giant brownies. That way we don't have to cook outside."

"We could just light the camp stove a few times during the night to warm things up," Ember suggested.

"And wake up dead from carbon monoxide poisoning?"

"Oh, yeah," Ember said, appearing mildly chagrined. "Guess I should have paid more attention in science class."

"Ya think?"

"Although..." she said, a smirk taking hold on one corner of her mouth, "technically you can't wake up dead."

"Smart-ass." Skyy forced her frozen knees to bend and stood.

"Can I drive?" Ember asked as she shut down the stove.

"Write me a two-page paper on the dangers of carbon monoxide poisoning and I'll think about it."

Canon stirred to beeps, buzzing, and an annoying someone who kept urging him to wake up. Gradually, his eyes focused on the curved ceiling track for the privacy curtain in the surgery center. He recognized the nurse bending over him as the one who checked him in earlier.

"Your surgery is all done, and you're in recovery." She raised the head of his bed several inches. "You did great. Would you like some apple or orange juice?"

Canon croaked an answer. By the time he sank back into the pillow, he wasn't sure which flavor he'd picked. It seemed like only minutes ago that his shoulder was being swabbed with disinfectant, the surgeon saying, *"We'll take good care of you today, Canon. Just relax."*

Real-life medical shows on TV fascinated him, so today he'd watched the operating room personnel with interest. Then the anesthesiologist asked Canon to count backward from one hundred. He might have made it to ninety-five.

Going from full awareness in the operating room to waking up in the bed was…well, disconcerting. He rubbed his forehead to get his brain firing. It wasn't at all like sleeping. In sleep, there is still an awareness of the bed, the sheets, sounds on the street—all things which give a sense of time passing. But anesthesia was as if a section of his memory had been snipped out and the ends spliced together like an old movie film. There was nothing in between.

The nurse returned, and Canon slowly drained the juice box while she checked his vitals. Outside his thin curtain, staff efficiently stowed supplies and talked about plans after work. His was the last surgery for the day, so by the time he finished the juice, the surgery center was mostly empty.

His doctor stopped in. "It was a badly torn muscle, Canon, but no damage to the rotator cuff. I was a little afraid going in that we'd find something worse, but it's all good news."

The bad news was Canon would have to wear a sling for two weeks, then physical therapy for a minimum of two months. He could go back to work on desk duty, but active duty required the doctor's release and re-qualifying at the shooting range since he was right-handed.

"Hey, Truax, ready to go workout at the gym?" Jimmy Rodrìguez stepped around the curtain and recoiled in mock horror. "Whoa, they said you'd look bad after surgery, but I didn't expect this."

Canon laughed. "This is the improved me. Should have seen me five minutes ago."

"Too bad they didn't slip in some plastic surgery, bro." He held his hands up palms out. "I'm just sayin'."

J-Rod—as everyone in the division called him because he hated it—gave Canon a ride home, first swinging by the pharmacy for pain meds he hoped he wouldn't need.

"I'll buzz you tomorrow—make sure you're still alive," Jimmy promised as he left.

Canon sank into his easy chair, but then realized he couldn't work the reclining lever on the right side. With a sigh, he struggled to his feet and paced across the room and back, wondering again if the anesthesiologist had juiced him with a stimulant to wake him after the surgery. Other than a dull ache, his shoulder didn't hurt at all, and mentally it was like he'd had the best sleep of his life and a drip line of high-octane caffeine.

He itched to do something and pulled the window curtains aside. The greenbelt of plants and shrubs didn't hide the building several yards across the narrow divider. The view never improved, not even in the dark.

His apartment, with its off-white walls, white appliances,

beige carpeting, and perpetually musty odor was probably identical to its eighty or so twins in the complex. For Canon, it was primarily sleeping quarters, and not even that while he was cross-training in San Diego where he'd been bunking with one of the single deputies.

Work was his stimulation, and that was off the table for a few weeks. When he'd been down with the flu last spring, he made the mistake of watching daytime television. *Please, God, never again.*

Looking around at the sparse furniture, he realized he hadn't planned his recovery very well. He'd go nuts if he stayed here for more than a day.

Jimmy had put the pain medication on the kitchen bar. If Canon took half of a pain pill tonight to ensure a good night's sleep, then tomorrow…

He picked up his phone and pulled up his brother's contact.

CANON:

Hey, Mart. Survived the surgery. Home 10 mins & already bored out of my mind.

MART:

:-) Glad to hear. Sorry 4 not being there. Can come in a couple days if u want.

CANON:

No need. Driving to the cabin tomorrow.

MART:

Cleared to drive already?

CANON:

I'm a law enforcement professional.

MART:

Doesn't make u smart, but OK. No drugs and driving.

Canon fielded Mart's questions about the surgeon's repair and assured him again he wouldn't make the drive if he wasn't up to it. Then Mart said they had a call at the fire station and had to go.

MART:

Meet u there Thurs nite if I can. Say hi to radio chick for me.

Canon checked the time. Still hours until the *Night Thoughts* show. Should he stay up? What with work, the injury, and the surgery, he hadn't communicated with Skyy in days. But there were no messages from her, either. He was probably one of many listeners with whom she occasionally traded messages.

His stomach growled, reminding him he hadn't eaten since last night. An apple juice box didn't count. One good thing about this apartment, it was within walking distance of Ms. Mimi's Thai.

He was struggling to get his coat around his shoulders when the first drops of rain peppered the apartment window. The weather forecasters were predicting widespread rain from a monster front pushing out of the northwest. Evidently, it had arrived, and walking a quarter mile in the rain and wind didn't sound fun. He sloughed off the jacket and rummaged through a stack of menus on the kitchen bar.

Good thing Ms. Mimi's Thai delivered.

CHAPTER 12

An hour before show time, Skyy tore open a new box of tissues. Her nose was draining like Niagara Falls, and her throat felt like a hand was squeezing it shut. It might have been the pine pollen or the cold, but it was nasty. A few drops of that icy date shake would feel so good.

"My voice is a mess," she whispered to Ember. "I might have to resort to a lot of music tonight. Let's get set up."

The camp's Wi-Fi was as strong as advertised, and they set up her compact operation in the trailer. Although their new electric heater whirred quietly and filled the space with warm air, the aluminum walls radiated cold as the outside temperature continued to plummet. She massaged her tender throat. Sleeping tonight would be a challenge.

Ten minutes before show time, Skyy opened her mouth to ask Ember to pass her water bottle. No sound came out. Ember's eyes went wide.

Skyy typed into her show notes window and turned the laptop for Ember to see.

"I have to tell Big Jer I can't do the show."

Ember shook her head. "I can do it." She sat up straighter and cleared her throat.

Skyy raised her brows.

"You do the technical part," Ember said. "I'll do the discussion. Where are your notes?"

Skyy scrolled to the top of the show notes and Ember began reading.

Two minutes before the show, Skyy's phone chimed. A direct message from the Black Owl Radio board.

Can't stay awake for your show. Pain meds knocking me out. - **Canon**

Pain meds? Skyy recalled her earlier feeling of unease.

What happened? - **Skyy**
Surgery. - **Canon**
r u ok? - **Skyy**

She stared at the tiny screen, willing a better explanation to appear. Then the music started for the show, and Ember pulled the microphone close.

"Hi, all. You're listening to Skyy D at Night on Black Owl Radio, and this is *Night Thoughts*. Hope you're having a good evening. I'm Ember, sitting in for Skyy D who has a touch of laryngitis. But don't worry, she's right here in case I goof up. Thanks for dropping in for our ramblings and to hear some great music from independent artists all over the world."

Skyy glanced at the girl. She'd nailed the intro word-for-word, and it wasn't written anywhere on-screen.

"Our first group is Their There out of San Francisco, with their new release, 'Jail Time.' That's appropriate, because our topic tonight is how do you know if he's a good guy, or if he should be imprisoned for life? We've all dated creeps. And yes, for you guys out there, girls can be creepy too.

Remember those mean girls in high school? Well, some just grow older, not better. How do you know if you've got a keeper to take home to mom, or a *Fatal Attraction* psycho that will boil up a bunny rabbit in your kitchen? And that movie *Pacific Heights* with Michael Keaton? Man, that was one sick dude."

Ember nodded to Skyy, and she clicked the link to signal Big Jerry. The music faded in.

"Sorry, that was kind of a crappy intro to—oops," she said when she realized the mic was still hot. Then she whispered, "Language, Ember. Language."

Skyy laughed silently, knowing even Ember's whisper came through on air.

Ember blew out a breath and spoke into the mic. "All righty. Let's listen to Their There while I get my act together. Then we'll talk."

Skyy clicked the mute button.

"Whew." Ember fanned herself with her hand and switched off the space heater. "It's kind of intense knowing you're speaking to millions of listeners."

Skyy smiled and typed *More like thousands, but you did fantastic!*

Ember grinned ear to ear. She squirmed on her bottom. "I could get used to this."

Skyy typed *Back off, girl.* But she couldn't hide her own grin. She hadn't realized what a natural radio voice Ember had. The rest of the show would be her proving ground. A red indicator flashed the end of the song. She clicked the mic button when Ember nodded.

"So, how do you know if the person you're interested in is a winner or a wacko? BT in Ohio says background checks are cheap and worth it. One girl he met online turned out to be a check forger with a long record. Her MO was to date a guy long enough to get a copy of his signature and a book of blank checks. Then, *shopping spree!*

"Caitlin in Seattle agrees, and says her friends wouldn't think of buying a car without checking its accident record, so why shouldn't dates be investigated?"

Skyy typed *Anyone else want to share more experiences using background checks?* Ember read the question for the listeners.

Over the next hour, Ember touched on the pros and cons of background checks that Skyy had found. Skyy coached her to slow down when she got excited and began speaking too quickly, and had her relax to mellow out her voice, which wasn't as naturally deep as Skyy's. Tone was part of the trademark of *Night Thoughts,* soothing and calming in contrast to the frenzy of a society bent on fast and noisy.

Ember caught on quickly, deftly fielding comments about how to stay safe on first meets, seeking up or down votes from friends, and reading warning signs. Some listeners wanted to know how to handle guys who wouldn't get a job or commit, but that was a bigger topic Skyy, via Ember, promised for a future show. Ember brought the discussion back on track, recommending using a cell phone to record tense situations, if legal in their state. And always having an escape plan.

"All right," Ember said as the show clock counted down toward zero. "It's been great hearing from you all tonight. Skyy D will be back for Friday's show—we hope—so tune in. Same time, same place, right here on Black Owl Radio. And, as always, be sure to send in music requests and topics you'd like to hear on future shows.

"You've been listening to *Night Thoughts*. This is Ember saying good night for Skyy D. Stay safe out there."

The *off-air* notice popped up from Big Jerry. Ember clicked the mute button to be safe.

"Great job!" Skyy typed on the screen. *"You're a natural."*

"Thanks," Ember said, grinning. "That was fun!"

As Ember bounced in post-show high, Skyy's last threads of energy drained away like the flick of a switch. "Oh, man," she wheezed, sagging forward.

"Skyy? Are you all right?"

"Sleep," she breathed, scooting down into her sleeping bag. She didn't care about closing down the equipment or stowing it away. Her throat—largely forgotten while concentrating the past hour—reasserted its raw presence.

One of the overhead lights went out, and she was vaguely aware of Ember exiting the trailer. If she came back, Skyy didn't know.

CHAPTER 13

WEDNESDAY SLOWLY GROUND BY IN AN ALTERNATING CYCLE OF shivering and sweating as rain and occasional hail pelted Skyy's metal home. Someone had reamed her throat with a toilet brush during the night, and swallowing the tiny sips of water Ember brought her was like drinking acid.

In the afternoon, she forced on her shoes and coat and headed across the campground toward the bathroom building. If she thought the air inside the teardrop was cold, it was nothing compared to the frigid blasts bending the pine trees and propelling their needles through the air like green daggers.

The temperature inside the campground bathroom wasn't any warmer. Numerous vents mounted at the top of the walls —which were perfect for bleeding away the heat of summer —poured in outside air, chilling tile countertops, floors, and toilet seats. Warmth from the single wall heater in the corner dissipated as quickly as it came out. She ran her hands under the sink's hot water before braving the refrigerated stall.

Several torturous minutes later, she crawled back inside the trailer, kicked off her shoes, and slithered deep into her sleeping bag. She wasn't sure if curling into a ball helped, but she tucked her knees to her chest. One Christmas when she was little, a kind neighbor gave her and Vance down comforters. They were too hot to use on any but the coldest nights, and she learned why ducks did fine in freezing water. Her parents donated the comforters to Goodwill when they moved south a year later. Skyy wished for one now.

If this followed the typical path of a virus, coughing would start soon. That and the persistent shivers might finish her off for good.

Ember opened the trailer door every couple of hours to check on her, bringing with her a swirling mist of freezing air. She had moved her sleeping bag to the car after the radio show, saying they couldn't both get sick. Skyy didn't have the energy to ask what the girl was doing to pass the time, what she was eating. *If* she was eating. Amelia Oso would not be pleased.

Their plan from before the show yesterday was to leave the camp this morning and drive somewhere warmer. San Diego was less than an hour away. Paradise, even in winter. Everyone wore shorts—she'd seen the pictures. Pristine beaches, sailboats on Mission Bay, swaying palm trees, the signature red tile roofs of Hotel del Coronado. What she wouldn't give to feel the sun on her face.

Instead, she slid the electric heater closer and closed her eyes. The warm air was a soft breeze, gently buffeting her eyelashes. She dreamed of San Diego on a summer day.

"Wake up, Skyy. We're getting out of here." Ember poked Skyy's shoulder, but she didn't stir.

"Here, let me."

Ember held the trailer door as the camp host reached in

and dragged Skyy's sleeping bag across the floor with her in it. The man was older, but wiry and stronger than he looked. Working together, he and Ember carried Skyy to the Jeep. Ember stretched the shoulder belt across the sleeping bag and latched it.

"Thanks," she said to the man. "And for your help hitching up too."

"No problem. You got the directions to the clinic?" When Ember held up the paper he'd given her, he gave a little wave, then ducked his head into the wind and headed for the warmth of his big trailer.

After one last walk around making sure they hadn't left anything, Ember climbed into the driver's seat.

"You can do this." She dried her palms on her jeans, then started the engine. She'd been watching the routine as Skyy started and stopped, applied and released the emergency brake, and shifted the automatic transmission. Skyy had let Ember move the car forward a few feet after unhitching, and once she'd backed it up to the trailer as Skyy guided her.

How hard could it be?

"Just like Xbox," she mumbled, shifting into drive and releasing the brake.

The Cherokee rolled forward, off the level parking pad and onto the road circling the camp. She straightened the wheel, then pressed the gas pedal. The car surged ahead.

"Whoa," she said, lifting her right foot. The Jeep slowed a little. She tried again, this time applying lighter pressure to the gas pedal.

For the next fifteen minutes, she drove around the camp loops, then ventured onto the access roads. Before braving the Interstate, she pulled into the parking lot of a closed restaurant and practiced making turns, getting a feel for how the trailer followed and how much force to use on the brake pedal.

Driving around two side streets had her palms sweating again. The parked cars were so close! But at least they weren't moving. It would be even harder when out on the highway with cars and trucks passing her.

Fortunately, the clinic was only twelve miles down the Interstate. Of course, that meant dealing with traffic, stoplights, turn lanes, and maybe cops.

But her plan was simple: Get Skyy to a doctor and get some meds so she could get better.

After that, Ember needed help.

And she knew who to call.

CHAPTER 14

CANON ROSE LATE THURSDAY MORNING, HIS BODY PROTESTING the very thought of moving toward the side of the bed and getting up. The coffee maker had finished its cycle over an hour ago, permeating the cold air with its enticing aroma.

"Time to get moving, Truax." He gritted his teeth and swung his feet to the floor. His shoulder—actually, his whole upper body—had stiffened during sleep, and it took a while to pull on some sweats.

He'd been a fool to make the drive so soon after surgery, and the intermittent heavy rain hadn't helped. At the halfway point he even considered stopping overnight, something he'd never done. But the overwhelming pull of the cabin kept him going mile after mile until he reached the turnoff to Storm Lake.

He shook a dead cricket out of a pair of fleece-lined booties Mart gave him last year and stuffed his feet into them.

In the kitchen, he downed half of a pain pill with a sip of coffee. Although overheated while he slept, it was still vastly superior to the brew at headquarters. He added some milk and sugar, as much for the calories as to mellow the taste.

Outside the front window, thin cirrus clouds dimmed the morning sun as they scuttled east, and the choppy, steel-gray lake surface warned away all but three or four brave boaters. This was the reprieve forecasters promised before the bigger storm late tonight.

It was stupid, but he checked his phone again. The ringer volume was set at high, so he would have heard any incoming message. The only one was an apology from Mart that he pulled an extra shift due to one of his buddies going on the disabled roster. Mart couldn't come until Saturday, and even that was iffy. That wasn't a worry. Canon had enough wood split and stacked to last until summer. It wasn't Mart he wanted to hear from.

A month ago, he found a website where he could schedule recordings of *Night Thoughts,* and he was able to play back Tuesday's show as he drove. The fill-in girl, Ember, sounded young, but she had a good radio voice and an easy-going presence. Although Canon missed Skyy's sexy alto, knowing she was in the studio with Ember made it better.

Wind whistled around the cabin's exterior and whipped the tall pines out front. Would the storm impact Skyy? He had no idea if she was nearby or far away. He'd posted a message yesterday in the middle of the afternoon, complimenting Ember and asking Skyy how she was doing. No response.

His stomach rumbled, reminding him his last meal had been on the road yesterday. It was either canned chili for brunch or drive to Peg's Waffle House in Deer Cove. With rain on the way, he needed to stock up on groceries so he could hunker down for a few days. He slipped his good arm into his jacket and pulled it around his right shoulder, leaving his right arm and sling against his chest. The coat wasn't zipped, but this way he could use his fingers.

"Oh, man," he said, breathing deeply when he stepped outside. The crisp air smelled of fresh water, pine, and woodsmoke. It was hard to believe he'd been sweating and lugging bundles of marijuana on the southern border just a few days ago. The fragrant lake aromas cleansed the past and promised adventure. Perhaps a little risk. Despite his aching shoulder, he couldn't help but savor nature's constant renewal.

The truck upholstery, stiff and brittle from the night's cold, creaked as he slid in. He could relate.

He drove one-handed toward Deer Cove. Midmorning now, the parking lot in front of Bibs' Beauty Barn was full when he passed, and he smiled at memories of playing in the corner while his mom got her hair done. Bibs and her sister, Irene, were characters of the first order, arguing with each other about everything from customers' hair styles to which one would die first. Bibs propelled them around the lake in a 70s-era Buick, which commanded the first parking slot by the big barn.

In town, Peg's, as always, had people milling out the door. He drove past and parked. If he was lucky, he could score a single stool at the counter.

As he opened the truck door and stepped out, his cell phone chimed. He was expecting another text from Mart, but this alert tone was different. It was the one he set for messages from Black Owl Radio. He clicked the direct message.

Canon Truax. This is Ember, Skyy's friend. She needs you. Can you help? - **Ember**

Ember flexed her fingers one hand at a time, working them until the white disappeared from her hurting knuckles. Who knew driving was so stressful? Especially pulling a trailer.

Traffic around San Diego and L.A. had been insane, and she had only skirted the edges. Now that she was out of it, she vowed to never go near Southern California again.

But Skyy had needed a doctor, and there wasn't one up on the mountain in Pine Valley. After begging some sample meds from the urgent care clinic doctor—and receiving in turn a stern admonition for Ember to keep her friend hydrated—the nurse helped them back into the car. Skyy was asleep in the passenger seat before Ember climbed behind the wheel.

That had been hours ago—hours of tense driving that set her shoulders and neck on fire. She rolled her head, which helped for two seconds.

She glanced over where her friend slept curled against the passenger door. The headlights of an oncoming car lit Skyy's face, and Ember hoped her pale complexion was a trick of the stark light and not her actual pallor.

The approaching vehicle grew larger and larger, its lights high off the ground. A big rig. Ember slowed and edged right, tightening her grip and holding the wheel straight as the truck and huge trailer flew past. Its wake pushed the Cherokee and trailer toward the shoulder of the two-lane road, but she eased it back into the center of the lane, not making the same mistake as earlier when she over corrected and swerved all over. She blew out a breath and flipped on the high beams. Her knuckles ached and were even whiter than before.

After the clinic visit, she thought about finding another place to camp. But according to the radio, a big storm was barreling onto the coast of California, and the thought of setting up camp in the rain was *way* unappealing. So instead, she'd used Skyy's phone and sent a message through Black Owl Radio to the cop hottie. She included Skyy's cell number so they could text directly. Truax sent back his own number.

As they came to a highway intersection, Ember pulled off onto the gravel shoulder to review the directions in Truax's last text. A low murmur escaped Skyy's chapped lips, and Ember touched the back of her hand to Skyy's forehead. It felt warm, but not burning up. Maybe the medicine was working.

It seemed like they had been traveling on back roads for hours, dodging trucks and squished skunks, always on the lookout for the Highway Patrol. Why did Truax have to live in the middle of nowhere?

"This lake better be worth it," she said, as fat raindrops began spattering the windshield. In seconds it rose to a drumming that drowned out the idling car engine. The storm had arrived. "Great."

Ember played with the windshield wiper control until they were on high speed, checked the side mirror, and turned toward Storm Lake.

"Okay," she muttered as she drove into the downpour, "you can do this."

The headlights pierced all of twenty feet, and the center line disappeared on shiny pavement. The cop hottie said it was about twenty-five miles from this turn. Limited by the rain and dark, it would take her another hour.

She took a deep breath and exhaled. "The lake and you *both* better be worth it, Truax."

Of course, Skyy would kill her once she woke up—at least boot her to the side of the road. But how bad could this go? Even if this guy wasn't dating material, he was a cop, not a creeper. He seemed like a nice guy. And those abs…

She thought of the *Night Thoughts* show when Truax called in. One phone call and a few traded messages. It wasn't much to work with in judging a person's character.

Surely police departments did background checks before they hired cops.

CHAPTER 15

CANON PACED THE SMALL LIVING ROOM, THEN OPENED THE front door and walked out on the covered porch for the fifth time. His breath came out in misty clouds, quickly dispersed by the twisting wet air. Rain had been falling from the roof edge in a solid wall for over two hours, dropping onto the bed of river rocks he and Mart had wheelbarrowed into place two summers ago. They could have installed a rain gutter, but thought the sound of water hitting the rocks would be a cool effect, especially when sitting under the sheltered porch around the chiminea. Usually it worked that way.

But this storm was a beast, dumping more rain than any in years. Water splashed all over the skirt of the house, onto the deck, and occasionally right up to the front door.

The house faced southeast, giving a grand view the length of Storm Lake when the weather was clear. He walked to the right end of the porch and looked up the driveway to the road above and behind the house. No sign of headlights, though he wouldn't have much warning in this storm.

According to his watch, it was 1:17 a.m. They should be here by now, but he knew anything could have happened: a downed tree, mudslide or rocks on the road, or accidents. That last had him checking road websites on his phone.

A gust disrupted the cascade, shoving it onto the deck and soaking his pants and boots before he could hop back against the wall. Maybe a gutter wouldn't be a bad idea. A big gutter.

He was about to go back inside when dim headlights appeared at the top of the driveway, then halted there, shining down the graded path that must look like a river to the driver. Canon pulled up his hood, switched on his brightest flashlight, and stepped into the torrent.

If not for the bill of his ball cap, the rain would have blinded him. Some drops stung his cheeks, and he knew it might begin hailing any second. He hurried up the slippery driveway, flashing the light ahead so the driver would see him coming. When he reached the SUV, the driver window lowered an inch.

"Canon Truax?" the female driver asked.

His flashlight glared off the wet glass, but the small opening gave a hint of bloodshot eyes and sagging shoulders. And maybe a touch of fear. He couldn't blame her…meeting a stranger at night in a raging storm.

Another person—Skyy, he assumed—was a dark bundle in the passenger seat, her face turned away.

"You must be Ember," he said to the driver who looked like she belonged in middle school, not towing a trailer through a monsoon. He couldn't help wondering if she was sitting on a phone book. She nodded as she peeled her grip off the steering wheel and flexed trembling fingers. Deep creases in her forehead broadcast her total exhaustion, and he was afraid she'd crash right there if he didn't get her inside. "Are you okay to drive down?"

She closed her eyes for a few seconds, then nodded again.

"There's a pull-through carport along the rear of the

house." He directed the flashlight toward it, but the beam was lost before ever reaching the house. He could barely see the light by the back door, and he knew where to look. "You'll see it when you get closer. I'll lead you with my flashlight."

Rivulets of mud tumbled egg-sized rocks over his boots as Canon slipped and slid ahead of the car. The seventy-five-foot driveway wasn't that steep, but the ground had exceeded its saturation point and everything now was runoff. The hill on the opposite side of the main road was giving up anything not firmly rooted. He made a mental note to talk with Mart about a way to divert the natural flow from coming right down their driveway.

He finally reached the packed gravel close to the house. It was flatter here, and he led Ember in a wide left turn around a stand of four pines and into the carport along the back of the house. His movement triggered the security light on the corner, illuminating the shelter.

Here, too, water fell in a sheet off the carport's roof, but the concrete pad remained relatively dry. He had already moved his pickup out the far end and had squeezed the ATV tight against the house wall.

Canon stood aside as the girl nosed the Jeep and trailer into the space. She sat up straight in the seat, trying to see where the front of the car was, and Canon motioned her forward until the whole car and most of the trailer were under the shelter. The Jeep was a little too far from the house, catching spray from the roof's edge, but he knew better than to have the girl back up and try again.

Ember staggered out, beating Canon to the passenger door and opening it. "We have to get Skyy inside. She's really sick." Ember wedged her hands under Skyy as if to lift her. It would have been funny if not so serious a situation.

Canon explained about the surgery on his right shoulder.

"Start with her feet. You'll have to get her up, then turn her so I can get my left arm around her waist."

The girl was willing, but drunk on her feet. They roused Skyy enough to stand while Canon got his arm around her. Her eyes never opened as he half dragged her to the back door and up the two concrete steps.

"Second door on the left," Canon said once inside the back door. Together, he and Ember lowered the unconscious woman to the bed.

"Why is she so cold?" Canon asked as he slipped his arm from beneath Skyy. Her shirt had ridden up and the skin of her back was like chilled granite.

"The heater quit working a few hours ago," Ember said, pacing on the other side of the bed. "I thought it would start again, but then the outside temperature kept dropping and dropping. I didn't know what to do."

"Okay," he said, sensing the girl's near panic. "We need to get her warm. I think there's a down comforter or throw in the hall closet. See if you can find it while I change."

Even with the raincoat, his clothes were soaked and dripping, and he'd left a trail of wet muddy footprints from the back door into the bedroom. He grabbed a pair of jeans.

Not wanting to track mud into the bathroom, he stepped back outside. The storm turned the carport into a wind tunnel, rattling beach chairs and yard tools hanging on the wall and sweeping rain from one end to the other. If anything, the downpour had intensified in the last few minutes. The tarp enclosing the end of the woodpile lean-to snapped like a schooner sail, and water was pooling under the Jeep.

Before he removed his boots, Canon ran around to the Cherokee's still open driver's door. He switched off the headlights, swiped a puddle growing on the seat, and closed the door. He'd have to put a heater and fan in it tomorrow to dry things out.

He huddled on the dry back steps, shucking his boots and stripping to his boxers. The hand on the big thermometer on the wall hovered just above thirty-five degrees, confirming the cold front's arrival. He hung the dripping jacket on a hook, followed by his flannel shirt. Getting the dry jeans on over his wet legs had him cursing his bum arm. Socks would have to wait until he dried his feet and wiped the muddy floor.

Back inside, he deposited the boots and soaked clothing in the laundry room sink. When he stepped into the hall, Ember stood there, clutching a puffy comforter. Her mouth was open, and her eyes flicked from his bandaged right shoulder to his bare chest. They lingered longer on his chest, which was nearly blue from cold.

"Sorry. I, uh…" he pointed to the bedroom, "need a shirt."

Her lips turned up at the corners. "No problem," she said, pivoting with a little hop and disappearing into the bedroom.

Since that's where his clothes were, Canon had no choice but to follow. Skyy hadn't moved, and he watched Ember cover her with the blanket. Getting a T-shirt and sweatshirt on with his injured arm took far longer than he wished, but he didn't ask the girl for help.

"I'll be right back," he said, exiting the room. He stuffed as many logs into the wood stove as it would hold. By the time he finished, the cast iron was so hot he had to shield his face as he pushed the glass door closed with a stick. But until he got the furnace fixed, it was the only heat in the house. He pulled over a small oscillating fan and set it to draw air past the stove and blow toward the hallway.

He wished for an old-fashioned hot water bottle like his grandmother had years ago, but he improvised by dampening two hand towels and microwaving each for a minute. When hot, he wrapped them in bath towels and took them to the bedroom. Ember sat on the bed, staring at her friend. Even from a few feet away, Canon could see Skyy shivering. He handed one bundle to Ember.

"Put this under the covers against her back," he said, "then lie down against it." When the girl was in place, he tucked the comforter around them.

He removed Skyy's tennis shoes and socks, then turned off the glaring overhead light. Sitting cross-legged on the end of the bed, he tucked Skyy's icy feet against his inner thigh, piled on the remaining hot towel bundle, and covered it with the comforter. Even through his jeans her feet felt like blocks of ice.

Idly, he wondered what the two women's story was, how Ember and Skyy were connected. Friends? Sisters? The younger girl's skin was darker, evidence of a different father or mother if they were related.

Her message and subsequent phone call had come as a complete surprise. Why had she called *him*? Surely they had family, a house somewhere, doctors. Yet, at the same time, it felt oddly natural. From all the hours listening to her show, he felt like he knew Skyy. And Ember seemed at ease. Her eyes were closed, and her breathing had slowed.

He shook his head. If Mart saw this scene, he would toss Canon's man card into the fireplace. His shoulder ached from the last couple of days, and the last hour hadn't helped. But, with Skyy's feet still shivering against his leg, no way was he moving to get more pills.

The red LED clock numbers clicked over to 2:19, and Canon let his own eyes close as nature's wet serenade drummed on the old shingles overhead.

CHAPTER 16

SKYY KEPT HER EYES CLOSED AS SHE SLOWLY GREW AWARE OF three things.

First, the shivers had decreased. Mild now compared to what had gone on for hours and hours, rattling her teeth and blurring her vision. She had a vague recollection of the car's vents blowing frigid air onto her legs and wondering why Ember didn't turn up the heater.

Second, the subtle scent of woodsmoke scraped her raw throat with every shallow breath, like inhaling burning coals. Maybe Ember had a campfire going wherever they had landed. If she could get her voice working, she would ask for a throat lozenge. She worked up a tiny bit of saliva and swallowed. That was a mistake. Whatever she was sick with still raged in her body.

The third thing she realized was the softness under her. This wasn't her sleeping bag. Was she in a hospital? But they didn't have smoky campfires.

She pried at her gluey eyelids. Her left eye cracked open first, then her right, but everything was a blurry wash of brown. Blinking helped, and gradually the film cleared. The brown became a knotty pine wall. Definitely not a hospital.

There was a slight movement in the bed and she looked down.

Okay. Four things. On her right side, the top of a man's head lay on the blanket level with her stomach.

"Hey," Ember said.

Skyy rolled her head left where Ember sat up and scooted back against the headboard.

"How do you feel?"

Skyy tried to answer, but only a hoarse wheeze came out. Ember left and returned a minute later with water and two pills.

"From the clinic," she said, and helped Skyy rise enough to swallow the pills. The water burned on its way down, but she emptied the glass. Even that minor exertion sent her head spinning. She closed her eyes for a moment, willing the room to settle.

"Are you hungry?" Ember asked. "Can I get you anything?"

Skyy opened one eye and pointed at the man's head. *Who is that*? she mouthed.

The girl stretched her arms in front of her, gripped like she was holding a gun. Then she fanned her face with one hand.

Skyy didn't have enough brain cells firing to play charades. She closed her eyes against a wave of nausea, urging the pills to stay put long enough to dissolve. Every joint and muscle ached, and nothing held still, not even with her eyes shut. The bed dipped and she felt Ember draw close. Warm breath whispered against Skyy's ear.

"That's Cop Hottie. And you know those abs? They're real."

When Canon woke, Skyy was turned away on her side. He listened for a minute to her breathing. It was slow and regular, no coughing or wet rumbles that could be a sign of worsening pneumonia. Ember was gone from the other side of the bed.

He gently rolled off the mattress and made his way to the kitchen. The girl had the coffeemaker open and was filling a measuring cup with water.

"Hey," she mumbled, blinking several times and squinting at the volume lines on the cup.

He nodded, watching as she put in a filter and grounds. She certainly had made herself at home. The kitchen window rattled as wind buffeted the cabin. Weather forecasters warned last night that the storm was stalling over the area, promising days of rain, some of it heavy, with a chance of rare snow. And after the storm blew through, the trailing weather front would be colder still. The wood floor was freezing under his bare feet, and the oscillating fan blew cold across his shins.

Leaving Ember to the coffee, he spent the next few minutes rebuilding the fire in the wood stove. By the time he finished, only two small logs remained in the bottom of the galvanized washtub used for storing wood and paper. Restocking meant a trip outside.

While the wood stove began radiating heat again, he stood at the front window watching the wide waterfall cascading off the front. It was after 9:30 in the morning, but the sun hadn't made an appearance, and dark gray clouds obscured the lake. Anyone who knew California weather understood how rare an event this was. And like the native he was, two days of wet had him ready to dry out. But it didn't look like sunshine was in the cards for a while.

"Do you have anything for a sore throat?" Ember asked,

coming up beside him at the window and handing him a cup of coffee.

"Are you getting sick too?" He eyed the cup in his hand, wondering how many germs had just leaped onto his skin.

"For Skyy," she said, wrapping her hands around her mug. "Her throat's pretty raw. I should have stopped, gotten her something. But..."

Her voice drifted off. Gone was last night's near manic energy and confidence bolstered by necessity. The girl's eyes were brimming with tears and the weight of responsibility.

"You did fine getting her here. Amazing, really, driving through this storm. Most people would have given up and stopped at a motel."

She dipped her head, concentrating on her coffee.

"We didn't have enough money. Or at least I didn't. And Skyy was so out of it with fever."

He glanced sideways at the girl while he sipped his coffee. He knew next to nothing about either of them. Was that why they were here? Two broke women with nowhere to go? Maybe they made a habit of looking for guys who were a sucker for pretty faces in distress.

"Have you known Skyy for a long time?" he asked. The girl was silent so long he began to wonder if she was making up a story.

"No." She blew on the mug—or it might have been a long sigh—then glared at him. "But she's my best friend, so don't hurt her or you'll be sorry." With that, she turned and walked into the bedroom. His bedroom.

Canon sighed. Good thing Mart wasn't here. He'd be laughing for hours.

Canon drove to the grocery store in Deer Cove, where he stocked up on cold and flu medications and three types of cough drops. The prices made him glad he'd paid off his credit card. For good measure, he added a dozen cans of soup to the cart, followed by saltines.

Usually he ate at Peg's or The Crab Shack for his big meal of the day, then filled in with snacks, but Skyy wouldn't be up for an outing for a while. He decided his meager groceries from yesterday weren't enough for three people, so he filled the cart with more mac and cheese, sliced turkey lunchmeat, eggs, bacon, a package of chicken breasts, ground beef, and two steaks. A package of Hamburger Helper went in. It might not be Ember and Skyy's favorite, but if not, Mart loved the stuff.

The produce department in the small store was a little ragged, but he found enough to pull together a few salads. A bag of apples and some oranges rounded out the fresh stuff. On the way to the checkout stand, he snagged a twelve pack of orange soda. He rarely drank the stuff, but maybe it would soothe Skyy's throat. Then he went back for some vanilla ice cream in case she wanted an orange float.

"Back again today, huh?" the woman checker asked as he piled the goods on the conveyor belt. "Looks like you've got friends staying over. A sick friend."

"Uh, yeah. Sort of." Sort of *staying* or sort of *friends*. He wasn't sure.

Rain drenched him again as he loaded the bags into the passenger side of the truck, and his wet clothing fogged up the windshield as he drove back on the slippery road. He hoped the refrigerator would hold everything.

After that, he'd have to bring in several loads of wood.

Canon was filling a canvas firewood sling when his cell phone rang. It was a miracle he heard it with the rain pounding on the roof of the lean-to at the edge of the carport. He and Mart had built the small structure to keep the woodpile dry, and it functioned well in normal weather.

"Truax," he answered, moving away from the splattering runoff.

"It's Captain Olenski. How's the shoulder?"

"I won't be tackling any bad guys soon, but it's improving a little each day."

"Good, good," Olenski said. From his tone and the rustling of papers, he sounded distracted. Or maybe he wasn't all that interested in Canon's healing. The man was difficult to read. "I just received word that three of those guys you fought with are having a pre-trial hearing at 9:30 Monday morning. The district attorney wants you there."

"Monday? I thought this would be weeks away."

"Turns out a few of these specific perps are high-value targets, and they've got big-money attorneys who are fast-tracking this like I've never seen. DEA is scrambling to get their case in order."

Canon explained he was six to eight hours away at Storm Lake.

"So…you're doing a little fishing on your vacation? That's what I'm paying you for?"

Canon stared at the water splashing off the carport. No one was doing any fishing in this storm, and technically he was out on disability, not working. He didn't think Olenski would appreciate the correction. "I—"

"Fly, drive—I don't care. Just get down here," Olenski growled. "You'll meet with prosecution attorneys Sunday morning to go over your testimony." Olenski shuffled more paperwork and recited an address, time to meet, and names of the attorneys. "This is a big case, Truax. Be there and don't screw it up."

Sunday. Canon slumped against the cabin's back wall. Disability or not, his time was not his own. And Olenski was right; this was an important case the DEA had been building for months before the opportune raid. Hundreds of man-hours of surveillance and planning, not to mention danger, had gone into the operation, and he didn't want to be responsible for weakening the prosecution story. They probably thought bringing in an injured officer recently out of the hospital would ingratiate them with the assigned judge.

He propped open the back door with his knee and lifted the bundle of firewood. Flying out of Mission Peak was a no-go. The airport canceled flights when it was barely misting. And driving south on a Friday afternoon in the rain would be a nightmare, especially with evening commuter traffic. He couldn't be taking any prescription pain pills while behind the wheel either, but if he started now, at least he could make it partway, get a good night's sleep somewhere, then make it to his L.A. apartment on Saturday. From there, it was a shorter hop to San Diego.

The firewood filled the metal bin to capacity. Ember could always go out for more if needed. He was about to sit down for a minute, when his phone dinged with an alert from KTLA news in Los Angeles. There were localized mudslides and flooding on parts of the 101 Freeway through Santa Barbara and Ventura. Sighing, he stood. He needed to get on the road and through there fast.

Now he just had to figure out what to do about two virtual strangers staying in his house. And he still hadn't talked to Skyy.

CHAPTER 17

An hour after Canon left for San Diego, Ember paced the living room while the rain beat relentlessly on the roof. She was used to roaming Tucson whenever she wanted, being outside, doing things. Camping with Skyy had been great until the weather turned cold. Even scrubbing toilets at BCJ sounded…

She shuddered. No need to get crazy.

Everything was ready for tonight. Big Jerry didn't need to know that she, not Skyy, would be doing *Night Thoughts*. Skyy was still sleeping, but seemed to be resting easier.

"Just an hour or two," she said, deciding. "Then I'll come back and get ready for the show." On her way out, she grabbed an umbrella from the hook by the back door.

Before he left, Canon had helped her unhitch the trailer and set up their portable heater and a fan inside the Cherokee to dry out the seats and floor mats. Heavenly warmth poured out as Ember opened the door, felt the carpet, and pressed her hand into the driver's seat. Warm and dry.

It didn't take long for the Cherokee to cool on the drive to town, but it was a lot better than the previous trip. On a whim, she parked on Main Street across from Peg's Waffle House. The thick clouds and rain made it seem later than it was, but all the businesses were still open. Their lights cast a magical feel to the village as she unfurled the umbrella and jogged across the street.

As soon as she opened the restaurant door, she nearly passed out from the delicious smells. Maple syrup practically dripped from the woodwork.

"Just one of you, hon, or are there more coming?" The woman—a waitress by the name of Pam, if her apron was accurate—was in her sixties, had frizzy hair, and appeared flustered as an even older waitress scooted behind her balancing two overflowing platters of food on her way to a busy dining room.

"I was—"

"Gotta be honest with you," Pam said, "it's going to be a bit of a wait. About thirty or forty minutes. We've got plenty of tables, but two of our cooks aren't here because of the road closure."

"Oh," Ember said. "I didn't know about that."

"Just happened a while ago. Landslide blocked a section. They're saying tomorrow but won't commit."

Ember nodded. She wondered if Canon had made it through, and then realized that if he did, he might not even know about the closure.

A man with a white chef's hat came up and whispered in Pam's ear, then headed back to the kitchen.

"Well," Pam said, "it seems like we're out of batter for waffles and pancakes. Our delivery truck was delayed from yesterday and now it's stuck on the other side of the road closure. Hope you like eggs and bacon."

"We're out of eggs!" a voice shouted from the kitchen.

"Pam?" A young waitress came up beside her holding up a credit card and meal ticket. "I was trying to run this, but our phone line is dead. What should I do?"

Pam rubbed her forehead. "If it's not one thing…"

"Actually," Ember said, "I'm looking for a job. Do you have any openings?"

Sixty seconds later, Ember was back on the sidewalk. Evidently servers at Peg's died of old age with syrup in their veins rather than retire. Although the way things were going inside, she wondered if Pam would croak from stress.

Honestly, Ember wasn't that disappointed. She'd worked at a burger joint in Tucson for a summer, and sometimes in her dreams she still smelled onions and French fry grease. Syrup and bacon, yummy as they were, might not be much better.

She worked her way down the few blocks of town, first one side, and then back up the other, hopscotching along on several *"you-might-try"* leads from well-meaning store personnel.

A restaurant called *Embers* had a gorgeous oval sign, where the bottom half was bright orange flames licking at suspended black lettering. It was only open for dinner, but she knocked, and a man answered. While amused that Ember's name matched the restaurant, he gave the same answer as the others: *"This is the slowest time of year."* Summer was a different story, but she couldn't wait that long.

Damp and discouraged, she climbed back into the Jeep and started the engine. Cold air blew on her legs, reminding her of the hours of driving while Skyy grew more and more ill.

With a sigh, she drove through town past all the shops she'd just visited. It wasn't exactly a metropolis, and employment options were limited. Still, it had a homey feel and a good variety of businesses suited to a busy lake community—come summer, at least.

Turning right at the far end of the businesses, she circled around the block. Cute bungalows and a few more stately homes occupied the street one back from Main. At least four had bed and breakfast signs out front, and she wondered what it would be like to stay in such a place. Dreaming aside, she and Skyy needed to find a place to rent. Or maybe just her if Skyy and Cop Hottie became a thing. That, of course, required the pair to actually meet and talk.

Ember continued to cruise the back streets, surprised there were so many houses and businesses. The farther she got from Main and the marina, the longer the streets were and the more buildings they held. A small boatyard had a handful of ski boats and a large garage building closed up and dark.

At the end of one of the streets, a sign marked the entrance to *Deer Cove RV* and advertised full hookups, monthly rates, showers, laundry, and cable TV. The paved driveway curved back into the trees, where most of the RV spaces she could see were empty. A classic camper painted yellow and white rested on a permanent foundation inside the entrance. A sign out front said *Office & Registration*, but it, too, was dark and locked. She would check back tomorrow about the cost. Camping in the teardrop for a month or two might be an option. Ember could even do it on her own if Skyy...

She was getting ahead of herself. There was no guarantee Skyy and Truax would even like each other. Still, he seemed like a good person. He helped her get Skyy into bed and helped take care of her, bought them groceries, hauled firewood. And the house was clean. What guy did all that if he was a jerk like Loser Boyfriend?

Ember turned around and drove up another street that had a commercial vibe. Finally, she passed a half-rounded metal building set back a hundred feet or so from the road. A Quonset Hut, she remembered from school.

The flat wood building front consisted mostly of a pair of tall, hinged doors. One was swung open, revealing a gaping interior and a row of fluorescent light fixtures running the length of the building. Above the doors, the weathered façade had *Deer Cove Auto* painted in faded white lettering. The graveled parking area in front had two newer cars and three that were older than Ember. A half-dozen wood pallets supported engines, transmissions, and other unrecognizable parts. Everything felt greasy, run down, and…sad. The place needed help.

At least it was open for business. She parked a few feet inside the chain-link gate and shut off the engine. Maybe she could wrangle some free advice on how to fix the Jeep's heater. Not that she knew anything about cars or trucks, but she'd learned long ago that asking never hurt. You just had to know when to run away if necessary.

Inside the building, a man in a gray mechanic's jumpsuit and reversed baseball cap straightened from under the hood of a small Toyota pickup. He waited just inside where it was dry, wiping his hands on a red rag as she approached.

"Nice Jeep," he said, nodding toward the Cherokee. "Those things are near bulletproof."

"Yeah," Ember pasting on her best smile. "Near."

"I'm Mark," he said. "What can I do for you?"

She looked around the yard again, seeing it from an outsider's point of view. Not one thing said *Welcome*. And if she'd learned anything at Backpacking, Coffee, and Jeans, it was to make a potential buyer feel comfortable. *"Draw them in, then sell."* Elliot had told her that dozens of times. It was the main reason for *Coffee* in the store name.

The worn board face of the Quonset desperately needed paint—a nice dove gray that wouldn't clash with the curved steel, trees, or neighborhood. And a sunny yellow on the business lettering would really make it pop. Maybe yellow window boxes with flowers. Even fake ones would do. Throw in movable privacy screens to hide the greasy parts pallets and some flower baskets hanging on the chain-link fence out front...

"Uh, miss?"

Ember snapped her attention back to the man and plastered on her best smile.

"Actually, I was...*am*...looking for a job."

He held up a hand to stop her before she could go further. "I don't—"

"Just hear me out. Here," she said, motioning him to step under her umbrella. "Come with me." Fortunately, the rain had let up, and she led him partway out into the yard.

"Hold this, please," she said, handing him the umbrella. Second rule of selling, according to Elliot, was to get the merchandise into the buyer's hand. Once there, they had a difficult time giving it back. In this case *she* was the merchandise, but the umbrella would do as a substitute. She lifted her arms toward the structure and opened them wide. Mark followed her gaze.

"Now," she said, "here's what I see."

The bedroom was dark when Skyy woke shivering. She fumbled for a bedside lamp, but knocked something to the floor. Seconds later the overhead light came on, and she threw her arm across her eyes.

"Sorry," Ember said. The light went off, and a few seconds later a softer light came on from the other side of the bed.

"What time is it?" Skyy pushed herself up against the headboard, taking stock of how she felt. She needed a shower, but the thought of getting wet with her chills caused her to shake even harder.

"Nearly 7:00 p.m."

Skyy pulled the blanket higher. Whatever she'd caught, it was a beast.

"Are you feeling any better?" Ember wisely stayed on the far side of the bed.

"Maybe." She couldn't remember ever being this sick. "Not really."

"At least your voice is back a little."

"Is the heat on?" Her shoulders were shaking, and she tucked the blanket around them.

"Sorry. I was gone for a while. I just added wood to the fireplace, so it will take a few minutes to warm up. Canon and I brought in a bunch—"

"Canon," Skyy whispered, searching the doorway and hall. "He's really here?"

"More like *we're* here," Ember said. "This is his house. Well, his and his brother's. See, their parents died a few years ago and—"

Skyy held up a hand. "Wait. How did we get here? And… where is here?" The questions were nearly too much to formulate in her muddled mind, but all she could think about was Amelia Oso depending on her to be in charge.

"Storm Lake, California." Ember rose and walked around the foot of the bed to the open doorway, as if maneuvering to an exit. "And I…sort of…drove."

"Without a license?" Skyy already knew Ember didn't have one, and she vaguely remembered the movement of the car. *Someone* other than Skyy had to have been driving. And since there were only the two of them on the road... Regardless, she couldn't stop the question or the Mom tone. Where did *that* come from? A throbbing was beginning right between her eyes, and she pinched the bridge of her nose.

"Well, *you* weren't in any shape." The girl's attitude was defensive, slightly belligerent, but she looked down. "I didn't get us killed or anything."

Had Skyy felt better, she would have laughed. Instead, she croaked, "How far?"

Ember inched further out the door. "A few hours."

"Hours?"

"Maybe ten." Ember glanced up briefly. "Or twelve." The girl was fully out into the hall now, her pink-tipped hair illuminated by the overhead light. It looked wet, as if she'd been out in the storm.

"And you pulled the trailer?"

Ember nodded and shuffled another inch.

Skyy wanted to ask about Canon Truax, where this lake was, where *he* was, but then Ember said, "I was scared you might die." The words came out as a breath, barely audible, but the fear they conveyed pierced Skyy's heart.

"Ember," she said, waiting until the girl hesitantly met her gaze. "I'm sorry. And thank you." Her head hurt and she felt like crap. All she wanted to do was curl up and pray for the hours to pass. But the girl's sudden grin was worth the effort of apologizing.

"It was scarier than I thought," Ember said, "especially in the dark. And the rain."

Rain? The girl drove through a storm? Skyy slid down in the covers and closed her eyes. "As soon as I'm better, we're getting your license." Her empty stomach growled. That was a good sign. If she could kick this fever, maybe tomorrow would be better. She could find out where they were, meet Cop Hottie for real, and figure out their—her and Ember's—next move.

CHAPTER 18

It was dark in the bedroom when Skyy's bladder prodded her awake. She located the lamp, this time without knocking anything over. The warm glow pushed away the darkness. She looked for her cell phone to check the time, but it wasn't anywhere in sight.

"Ember?" There was no answer. No man appeared, either.

Canon Truax. She shook her head. How had Ember pulled off finding him and getting them to his house? The girl was something else.

Cautiously, Skyy swung her legs off the bed and sat up, assessing her equilibrium. The T-shirt she wore was clammy from sweat, as were the sheets and pillowcase. But her head wasn't spinning. She touched her forehead. Cool. The fever had broken—at least for the moment. Maybe the worst was over.

The door to the hall was open, and across it was the bathroom she fuzzily recalled Ember helping her to. Skyy stood and headed to her goal.

Thankfully, the toilet seat wasn't too frigid, but she hurried just the same, then gasped at the icy tap water as she washed her hands. She hoped there was a water heater, because a shower was a must, not a want. But first she had to see if anyone else was in the house.

The hallway ran from the back door to the front of the house where it opened into a large space. The living room was on her left, a free-standing wood stove glowing as a low fire burned behind its glass door. She moved to it and turned, letting the radiating heat warm her back as she checked out the sofa, love seat, two chairs, tables and lamps that crowded the room. It felt homey, lived-in, a comfortable, put-your-feet-on-the-coffee-table kind of place to relax and laugh with friends.

A guy-sized flatscreen television was mounted in the corner opposite the fireplace. Beneath it, a small credenza held game controllers, a DVD player, and a row of movies. All action films, from what she could see without getting closer.

Two large windows filled most of the wall above the sofa, their view hidden behind closed horizontal blinds. Was this the view of the lake Canon Truax described in his messages?

An entry door divided the front wall of the house, and beyond it was a dining table with six chairs and corner windows giving views to both the front and side. Blinds didn't cover these, but the outside darkness transformed them into black mirrors. Her ghostly reflection rippled across the glass as she walked toward the dining area and into the open kitchen.

Under-cabinet lights bathed dark stone countertops, the only illumination in the front of the house. It was plenty to identify the typical appliances and wood cabinets stained a warm cherry. A simple coffeemaker held a prominent place to the right of the sink set under another dark window looking out the side of the house.

She opened the refrigerator. It was well stocked,

everything from milk to eggs to salad fixings. Although she needed to eat, nothing sounded good. Her stomach was the size of a shriveled walnut. Maybe after her shower.

When she closed the refrigerator door, a wall clock caught her attention. It read 1:33. Since it was dark outside, she had to assume it was the middle of the night. And if that were true, where was Ember?

Leaving the kitchen, she headed down the hall again, past the bathroom and her bedroom, and looked into a smaller bedroom on the left. Ember's duffel bag lay open at the foot of the bed, and her toothbrush and toothpaste sat atop a small chest of drawers. This was the only other bedroom. Which meant Canon Truax must be sleeping on the front sofa.

A muddy mat marked the back door at the end of the hall. She leaned close to the door glass and peered through. An outside porch light showed a concrete area with a sheltering roof. Rain dripped off the far edge in a constant fall. Her little trailer sat to the left, partially under the enclosure, its tongue jack resting on a block of wood. Her Jeep was gone and there was no sign of another vehicle.

Where were Ember and Canon? Her memory was intact enough to remember Ember had been here earlier—hours ago. She tried to shake off worry, hoping the girl wasn't driving all over when she didn't have a license. If a cop stopped her, he would impound the car.

Turning away from the cold glass, she noticed one more room on her right at the back of the house. She fumbled at the inside wall and found a light switch. An overhead fluorescent fixture flickered twice, then came to life, lighting up a long, narrow space occupied by a washer, dryer, utility sink, and water heater.

Although her energy was waning, Skyy stripped the sheets off her bed and got the washer started. If she was going to be clean, then so was the bedding. She hoped the water heater could keep up with both the washer and a shower at the same time.

The shower head blasted her sensitive skin with a little too much pressure, but it made washing her lank hair easier. Finally clean, Skyy dressed in her favorite sweat pants, a long-sleeved tee, and some thick socks she found in Truax's dresser.

Her body temperature fluctuated between hot and cold while she dried her hair. The virus might be losing its grip, but it had done a number on her, and she was pushing her limits being up so long. Once her hair was mostly dry, she collapsed on the living room sofa and sank into its hold. A soft throw slid off the back, and she pulled it around her shoulders against a sudden chill. Her eyes fell closed. Ten seconds later, the washer buzzed its end of cycle.

She squinted at the hallway. There were machines now that would both wash and dry without human intervention. When she got rich, she was buying one. She rose to transfer the load.

Sometime later, noise from the back door opening woke Skyy. She'd fallen asleep on the sofa. Shoes stomped on the mat, and the door closed.

"Skyy?" Ember said in a whisper.

"In here," she said, levering her body to a sitting position and rubbing some life back into her face. How could she still sleep after the last few days? The fire behind the glass was down to red coals, and the room had taken on a slight chill.

"Are you feeling better?" Ember said, coming into the room. There was hope in her voice. Relief. Skyy's tech bag was slung over her shoulder.

Skyy nodded. "I won't be running any marathons for a while, but I can stand up."

"I didn't know you were a runner," Ember said, easing the equipment bag to the floor.

"I'm not."

Ember grinned. "Well, you must be better if you're doing laundry," she said, thumbing toward the hall where the clothes dryer rumbled through its cycle. She stripped off her coat and knelt before the wood stove, then opened its glass door and began expertly fitting in chunks of wood from the pile in a galvanized washtub. The fuel caught and flamed, and Ember rubbed her hands. "Burr. It's freezing out there. Canon said we might get snow in the next few hours."

Skyy sat straighter, scooting down the sofa to be closer to the fire. "Where is he? I still haven't talked to him."

"He went to San Diego for some legal meetings. Hopes to be back Tuesday evening."

Tuesday? Skyy stared into the rising flames. The glass door seemed an apt reminder of her non-relationship with Canon Truax. Was she ever going to meet the man face to face? She turned back to Ember.

"And speaking of evening, where were you at this time of night?" She didn't add *young lady,* but she cringed at sounding like her mother—again.

Ember pivoted on her butt and hugged her knees to her chest. "I went into Deer Cove, the town here at the lake."

"And something was open?"

The girl tilted her head. "You don't realize this is Friday night, do you? Well, technically Saturday morning now." She jumped up and headed into the kitchen.

"The show!" Skyy started to rise, but then sank back. She'd missed *Night Thoughts*. Jerry would be...well, not furious—she'd never seen the man really mad. But he hated how his voice sounded on air and refused to fill in the one time she'd asked. She massaged her temples, imagining him trying to do a whole hour.

"Chill, girl. I covered it." Ember popped open an orange soda from the fridge and took a long swallow. "Ah, just like the hot old days in Tucson." She sank down by the fire again.

"You did the show?" Skyy asked.

Ember shrugged. "Wasn't that hard after last time. But I had to find Wi-Fi. There isn't any here at the house. Fortunately, DC Coffee's was wide open."

"What did Jerry say?"

The corner of Ember's mouth curved up. "I may have inadvertently let everyone think you were there with me, like last time." She tipped the soda can bottoms-up. "I mean if Jerry asks, which he probably won't because the show went great. You're welcome."

She crumpled the can, rose, and headed back to the kitchen. "I'm still thirsty. Want one?"

Before Skyy could answer, Ember returned with two sodas.

"Thanks," Skyy said, taking the offered can.

"Sure."

"I mean for the show, too. I owe you." She popped open the can and sighed as the cold orange liquid soothed her throat. "Did you have a topic for tonight?"

"New beginnings," Ember said. "I asked if people had a chance to change things up and start new, what would they do. It was interesting."

"Did you get any calls?" Usually a topic like that generated a few phone calls in addition to the message board.

"Some," Ember said, but didn't elaborate. "I should get a bicycle."

Skyy shook her head at the abrupt change of subject. "Why would you need a bike?"

"To get to my job at Deer Cove Auto. I start Monday."

"Job? How did—?"

"'Course if it's raining, maybe I can borrow the Jeep again. Mark said he could fix it, by the way."

Skyy's head was spinning now. Maybe it was a sugar rush from the soda on her empty stomach. "Did you get in an accident?"

"Of course not," Ember laughed. "I'm an excellent driver. But don't you remember how cold it was when we were driving? He said the heater core is probably clogged."

The girl spun into a jumbled monologue about how Canon put a fan and portable heater in the Jeep to dry it out because it was soaked—she didn't explain *how* it got wet—and how she also applied for some shifts at DC Coffee. Waitressing at a restaurant was way low on her list, but working with espresso machines sounded interesting. And, they had ice cream. Bonus!

"And while Mark's a good mechanic, he's lousy at answering the phone, record keeping, and following up on ordered parts and billing." She looked at Skyy and shrugged. "His words, not mine. The first thing I plan to do is use the shop power washer to clean the seriously disgusting bathroom." She shuddered.

Skyy set her soda can aside and leaned back on the soft cushion while Ember rattled on about how nice Conrad Langworth at the coffee shop was, his yummy special creations, and the cute shops in town. The girl's rapidly shifting topics taxed Skyy's ability to keep up, but she was familiar with the emotional high that always came after a good *Night Thoughts* show. Plus, it was refreshing to hear about anything after days lying in bed.

Ember was already putting down roots in the community, while Skyy had barely been out of the bedroom. There were other questions for which Skyy wanted answers. Where did Ember think they would live? And what was the absent Canon Truax like in person?

But as curious as she was, her body had other ideas. When Ember's manic energy finally drained away, the crackle of the fire filled the room with a hypnotic dance of light and sound. Skyy was too tired to ask anything except for help making the bed. Then she crawled between the clean sheets.

After Skyy crashed, Ember lay on her bed, staring at the white ceiling and listening to the crackling of the fireplace in the living room. It was nearly 3:00 in the morning. She should be exhausted.

Tonight's show focusing on new beginnings was more than an interesting topic, it was her personal new reality, her life. Which is why she picked it. And everything had gone really well—until that one phone call.

K, the girl who called when they were still in Tucson, called again. And naturally it was the one time Skyy wasn't there. When the girl began crying, saying she had to get out or she was going to die, Ember hadn't known what to say or do.

But right then the comments window flooded with message after message, page after page, all from one person: *Creeper*. They blinked away almost as fast as they came, but some lingered a few seconds, as if Big Jerry was deleting them manually. His automated scripts had failed.

Knowing he'd be busy for a minute or two, Ember quickly encouraged K to post her contact information, then moved on to the next caller. After K's emotional confession, discussing the new caller's weight loss goals felt decidedly mundane, but it had given her time to steady her heartbeat.

Too bad her heart was now seeking a rematch when it should be snoozing. She kicked off her blanket and went out to the kitchen bar. The dimmed under-cabinet lights bathed the room in a warm glow. Outside, the storm raged again, wind pressing against the windows and distorting their interior reflections.

*I'm in San Francisco. - **K***

That and a phone number had been the girl's message.

Beyond the pulsing heat and fragrant smoke of the fireplace, Ember caught the occasional scent of wet pine that seeped in gaps around the doors and windows. San Francisco wasn't that far north. Was K out in this tonight? Was she someplace safe?

Ember shook her head. The girl was no doubt a prostitute with a pimp. Although she might finally be inside this time of night, there was no place really safe.

The kitchen lights flared and dimmed, then returned to normal. Ember willed them to remain on, holding her breath and counting seconds. At thirty, she exhaled. Finding a flashlight and candles seemed like an excellent idea, so she began searching cupboards and drawers.

After K's first call in Tucson, Skyy mentioned she wished she could help the girl. Knowing that, didn't Ember pretty much have to encourage K to post a message with her contact info? It's what Skyy would have done. The message stream was private, so the public couldn't see the entry. Big Jerry could, but he would have been busy with other things, only scanning for the Creeper's posts, not the others. She hoped.

*I'm in San Francisco. - **K***

When Ember called the number, she'd gotten a generic

voicemail box. During subsequent songs, Ember called it twice again before braving to leave a message—with Skyy's cell number and a rough description of where they were. But Skyy was such a private person, just remembering divulging that info had sweat breaking out on Ember's upper lip again.

By the time she finished the show and signed off, K hadn't called back. And not long after that, a cell tower must have gone down, because Skyy's phone connectivity changed to *No service*.

"Ah ha," Ember said, spotting a fat candle and long butane lighter on a shelf. As she reached for the items, the kitchen lights blinked out, and cold blackness blanketed her. She froze, eyes wide, straining for light. Eventually, yellow flickering from the living room fire seeped around the corner, and she retrieved the candle. The lighter flicked to life, its flame wobbling as she touched it to the wick and the candle took over. She nearly extinguished it as she let out her breath.

The fire in the living room felt safer than the bedroom down the dark hallway. Too much like a horror movie. She settled on the sofa and wrapped herself in the throw. Again, she closed her eyes and listened to the rain being pushed sideways by the howling wind. The fire crackled a welcome counterpoint.

K lived without this comfort. But San Francisco was only a couple hundred miles north. Perhaps there was hope after all, and a chance for a new beginning. For both of them.

CHAPTER 19

SKYY WOKE SUNDAY, HER STOMACH FINALLY REQUESTING sustenance. At least she felt well enough to eat. The bedside lamp stayed dark when she turned the knob, and flipping the wall switch for the overhead had no effect. The power was off. Outside, the wind buffeted the cabin, howling around corners and whistling in cracks. She shivered and decided clothing was the first priority in the chilly room.

Her fashion-forward attire consisted of sweats and thick wool socks. She cinched and re-tied the drawstring around her waist to keep the sweat bottoms up, her belly button closer to her spine than it had been in years. She headed to the kitchen in search of food.

Instead, she found a note from Ember:

Gone to Sunday service at the little chapel in town, then working a shift at DC Coffee until 4. Power is out at the house, but on in town. Canned soup in pantry. Lighter for the gas stove is by the knife rack. — Ember

Skyy replaced the note. The girl had found two jobs and was attending church. Skyy hadn't yet ventured out of the cabin.

Her stomach growled enthusiastically at the promise of

soup. She used the butane lighter and ignited a burner on the stove, the blue flame pushing back the gloom. While waiting for some canned soup to heat, she sank onto a bar stool and rested her chin in her palm.

The rain was less intense, but swirling clouds surged across the ground in a misty gray blanket. The world could end just beyond the straight trunks of pine trees barely visible a few yards from the cabin, drop into an abyss like an episode of *The Twilight Zone*. She shuddered. Someone must have contact with the outside world. How could this place be so cut off?

The paltry effort of eating the soup and a few saltines had her dragging toward the sofa. Instead, she forced herself to first add wood to the stove, gratified when yellow flames danced higher and higher.

She wanted to keep her eyes open, wait for Ember's return. While exploration wasn't high on Skyy's priority list at the moment, she envied the girl's ability to get out and see things. Other than these few rooms and a glimpse outside, Skyy had no sense of direction or the surroundings. It was as if she'd been blindfolded and imprisoned in a remote cabin by an invisible kidnapper. She could be anywhere in the U.S.

Stupid, but that didn't make it less disconcerting. Her north-south bearings were scrambled.

Cold radiated from the picture window above the sofa, so she tucked the soft throw around her shoulders and closed her eyes once again. Maybe this was God's payback for badmouthing Tucson's relentless sun.

CHAPTER 20

MONDAY AFTERNOON, SKYY STOOD AT THE FRONT WINDOW, wincing as menacing clouds once more raked through the tall pines out front and churned the lake water to roiling dark steel. She hoped the trees had good roots. The promised snow hadn't arrived on Saturday or yesterday due to the moderating influence of the Pacific Ocean miles to the west. But, according to Ember, townspeople were holding hope for this afternoon and evening as a new front swooped down from Alaska.

The cell service and electricity at the cabin had remained off for the entire weekend. She and Ember saved the refrigerated and frozen food by moving it into large ice chests they found in the laundry room and carrying them outside. When the power came back on an hour ago, Skyy transferred all the food back inside.

That took all of ten minutes. Now, she was rapidly going stir-crazy. She scowled at the whitecaps. Feeling better had its disadvantages.

With Skyy's reluctant permission, Ember had taken the Jeep for her first day working at the auto repair shop. She also took Skyy's cell phone in case service worked in town. The house phone was still dead and being cut off from the world had her out of sorts. Her world was online, and she wasn't.

"First world problems, Delaney," she growled.

At least it wasn't raining, hadn't been for a couple of hours, though the air was heavy. She paced to the back door and surveyed the carport. The only remaining vehicle, a four-wheel ATV nudged against the house's rear wall, called to her. A set of keys with a Yamaha fob hung on a brass cup hook beside the door. The question was if it would start and remain running. Ember said Deer Cove wasn't far. However, getting stranded and walking might be a stretch after being sick.

Aware her indecision was burning the weak daylight, Skyy donned a couple more layers of clothing from her bag, then topped it off with a thick waterproof overcoat she found on a peg in the laundry room. The coat had man-sized gloves in the pockets, smelled of fresh air and pine, and covered her to mid-thigh. Her tennis shoes were a weak complement, as was the L.A. Dodgers baseball hat, also from the laundry room. They would have to do.

The cold slapped her face as she stepped outside, but she ducked her head against the wind and checked out the ATV. It had a full tank of gas and an electric start button. A girl Skyy had known as a teen in Florida had two brothers with similar models. She invited Skyy out to their ranch to go exploring. It only happened once, but that was the most fun she had that year—before they moved again.

She straddled the machine, gasping as her jeans hit the icy vinyl seat. The cold engine required some fiddling with the choke while cranking, but it soon roared to life and filled the carport with pungent exhaust. The wind quickly cleared away the fumes.

While the motor warmed up, Skyy tested the brake

controls, the lights, and transmission settings. She twisted the throttle and eased the machine through a tight circle in the carport, passed her little teardrop trailer, then bounced up the rutted driveway. Mud flew behind when the tires spun on the slick spots, but she made it up to the main road. At least she *thought* it was the main road. It was paved, but only one lane wide. And now that she was here, she realized she didn't know if Deer Cove was to the right or the left.

On a whim—but mostly because a stiff wind was blowing from the left—she turned right and accelerated. As freezing as the air was against her bare face, it felt great to be moving. She passed a handful of driveways leading to cabins nestled in the trees, but there were no cars on the road. Good thing, because the ATV didn't have a license plate and surely wasn't street-legal.

With each driveway she passed, the road narrowed, and after a winding three quarters of a mile or so, a pair of signs marked the end of the county-maintained road. Beyond the signs, asphalt transformed into gravel, the road ahead marked by two tracks where tires had compressed the soil so not even the weeds could break through. Vehicles were cautioned to proceed at their own risk. Deer Cove wasn't this direction.

Skyy made a U-turn and plowed into the stiff wind. She kept the ball cap as low as she could and still see the road, but the air stung her cheeks and reddened her nose. Regardless, it felt great to be outside, away from the confines of the cabin and bedroom.

A mile or so after passing all the cabins, including Canon's driveway, she passed a large barn on her right. The road widened here, and other roads led off to the right, but her eyes were watering and she didn't look or stop.

The swimming area that Ember had told her about had a

parking lot on the left. Deserted picnic tables, grills, and playground equipment dotted a grassy area at the edge of the lake. A little farther past the beach, a white building marked the beginning of town. The sign out front said DC Coffee. While Skyy had only been riding a short time, she needed something hot *right now!* She turned across the road and parked the four-wheeler on a patch of grass near the store's deserted patio. Her knees were stiff with cold as she climbed off.

A bell over the door tinkled as she entered, and scents of coffee and sugar washed over her. She breathed deeply and smiled, feeling truly alive for the first time in days. Coffee shops were familiar territory, and it was good to be back with the living.

Only two of the tables were occupied, and the raised bar with its line of round stools was empty. Skyy spun onto one and faced the counter, rubbing her hands. An older man with stark-white hair, matching two-day stubble, and bright blue eyes approached her.

"Nippy for an ATV ride." He nodded toward the windows overlooking the Yamaha.

"Sure is," she said, "but I had to get out for a bit."

"Looks a lot like the Truax machine. Might I assume you are Skyy Delaney?"

"And you must be Connie," she said. "Ember told me about you."

The corner of his mouth twitched. "Ember, yes. She's quite persuasive. I found myself offering her a job and thinking it was my idea all along. Almost gave her a raise before she left."

Skyy laughed.

"Don't tell her that," Connie warned, "or she might own this place by the end of the week."

No wonder Ember liked this man right off. Interesting, too, that he knew Canon Truax well enough to recognize the ATV. She fought the compulsion to ask him about the cop.

Conrad Langworth officially welcomed her to Deer Cove, and soon had her outfitted with a complimentary scone the size of a baseball mitt. He paired it with a hot drink topped with three inches of whipped cream. He claimed it was a light variety. Right.

"I heard you've been sick, so I don't want to overload your system."

As if the scone by itself wouldn't send her into a sugar coma. She closed her eyes as the first bite melted on her tongue. The pastry was full of sweet butter, lemon, and blueberries.

"Someone might have to drive me home," she said, breaking off another chunk and vowing she would save half of it for later. She hadn't even tried the drink yet.

"They might anyway," Connie said, lifting his chin toward the front windows. "It's beginning to rain."

Skyy spun on the stool. In the span of thirty seconds, small drops grew to medium size, then large, pelting the windows and bouncing off the patio tables as if trying to strip their white paint. The few pedestrians outside ducked heads and ran for cars or shop doorways.

Connie offered his phone, and Skyy called Ember for a ride whenever she finished at the auto repair. Relieved she wouldn't have to mount the ATV in the cold and wet, Skyy relaxed as Connie told how he'd branched out from his other shop in nearby Perilous Cove. At least seventy, he was as vibrant as a man in his forties, and his warm blue eyes reminded her of a summer afternoon.

"I like the warm dry air here at the lake," he said, "excepting today, of course."

Another couple rushed in to escape the rain and joined Skyy at the bar. As Connie fixed their orders, the three laughed at his stories about growing up in Hollywood and sneaking into the production lots with his friends.

"We kept trying to blend in with the paid extras so we could go see ourselves in the movies, but the security guards caught us every time and tossed us out. One of them finally called our parents, so we never made it onto the big screen."

She laughed again, then realized laughing had become a solitary exercise the last years. Sure, she laughed at the occasional online meme—by herself, or a funny post on the *Night Thoughts* page—by herself. Before she could go too far down *Poor Me Lane,* Ember came in and took the stool beside Skyy.

"That was fast," Skyy said, checking the wall clock at the end of the bar. "I didn't expect you for an hour."

"I bartered with Mark. Told him if I could leave early, I'd bring him a Cappuccino Blast tomorrow." She pointed at Skyy's plate. "What were you eating?"

Skyy looked down. Only a few crumbs remained on the plate where the giant scone had sat. Maybe it was her imagination, but she envisioned her blood sugar bouncing along the coffee shop's ceiling like a helium-filled balloon. She groaned. "I think that was lunch, dinner, and tomorrow's breakfast."

"I'll take one of those," Ember said to Connie. "Please," she added when Connie raised a brow.

"Coming right up."

"Did you ask him about using the Wi-Fi tomorrow night?" Ember whispered to Skyy.

Skyy rested her head in her hands. Now the room was for sure spinning. *Night Thoughts* was tomorrow, and she'd blanked on what day today was. Too much time being sick.

And when feeling better, dwelling on a certain cop. And overdosing on evil scones. She had to get her act together. The show required high-speed connectivity, and it was time to find some of her own. This tagging onto another's service wasn't fair to the person paying the bill.

Connie—like an ever-listening bartender—heard Ember's question. He tapped his chin with two fingers while Ember explained the need.

"Tell you what," he said. "You buy two drinks or scones a week, and I'll throw in all the Wi-Fi you can use. Twenty-four-seven access."

"We'll also need a key," Ember said matter-of-factly, then "What?" she exclaimed at Skyy's elbow in the ribs. "I'm already an employee. And we can't sit outside if it's like thirty degrees and snowing."

Connie went to the back room for a few seconds, then returned. Ember beamed as he slid a shiny brass key across the bar.

"If I'm missing any Cappuccino Blasts, I'm comin' after you, missy."

Ember saluted. "Yes, sir!" But she couldn't hide her big grin.

"By the way," Connie said, placing a phone note pad on the bar, "Canon called earlier and left a message on my machine here. Probably couldn't get through to you because of the cell towers and lines being down."

Skyy picked up the pink note.

Skyy & Ember -
Just checking in. If I get out of here early enough on
Tuesday, I'll be home late. Hope you're feeling better, Skyy.
Call me if anything comes up. - Canon

The shop door opened and closed a few times while Ember ate, each time flooding the room with colder air than the previous breach. It was growing dark outside, and everyone was excited about the prospect of snow, an evidently rare event at Storm Lake.

One time when the door opened, the freezing tide kept coming, eliciting a small chorus of *"close the door"* by those sitting at the tables. Skyy turned to face the front of the building.

A waif of a girl stood framed in the opening, one hand propping the door wide, the other clutching a small black trash bag at her side. Despite the freezing weather, she wore only a thin waist jacket over a tight mini-dress that ended more than a foot above her knees. The rain obliterated any style her ash-blond hair might have had, giving her a drowned-rat appearance. Water ran down her porcelain skin, forming a growing puddle on the tile floor around a pair of black high heels at least two sizes too large for her feet.

"Come in," Connie called, waving the girl forward. She remained where she was, eyes darting and connecting with each person in the room one at a time. Finally, her shoulders shook and her eyes fluttered, whether from cold or decision, Skyy couldn't tell.

"I'm looking for Skyy D," she said, her voice hitching in desperation. "She lives somewhere around here. Do any of you know her?"

Only Ember and Canon Truax knew the Skyy Delaney sitting on this barstool was Skyy D of *Night Thoughts*. Who—?

Ember's sharp intake had everyone, including Skyy, turning to her. Ember hopped off her stool and took a step forward.

"K?"

CHAPTER 21

Skyy glanced at Ember, then back at the girl in the doorway. *K*. The girl who had called in to *Night Thoughts* one time? How did this girl find out where Skyy was? Until a couple of days ago, *she* didn't even know.

The girl was staring at Ember. "You're Skyy D?"

Ember shook her head. "I'm Ember." She pointed at Skyy. "She's Skyy D."

Now it was beginning to make sense. Ember had done Friday's show by herself, and she'd obviously been a busy little cohost.

Skyy stepped forward, but stopped halfway across the room. The girl, shivering as she was, appeared ready to bolt right back into the freezing night at the first sign of aggression by anyone. Fortunately, everyone in the coffee shop was too engaged in the drama to make a sound. A couple held up cell phones, probably videoing the encounter.

"Hello, K," Skyy said, keeping her voice low and even. If this girl came from the life Skyy suspected she did, the last thing she wanted was some bubbly, phony enthusiasm. K was used to life on the streets. No one there was bubbly, not even friendly—unless they wanted something. "It's nice to finally meet you. Please, come in."

K didn't move, but her eyes betrayed a flash of longing. Skyy might not see that same expression on her own face in the mirror every morning, but she knew the feeling: a wanting of things beyond her reach, sometimes beyond what she felt she deserved. If she desired something too much, the disappointment of not gaining it would gouge deeper than never wanting it in the first place.

She remembered too well the first missed Thanksgiving with her parents and brother after her natural family imploded into a hot mess. So many Christmas trees and presents lost, July 4th backyard barbecues and sparklers that never happened. And Loser Boyfriend had made it clear he didn't want that either, at least not with her.

She sighed inwardly. Maybe she could do better with K, give the girl hope for a future far better than whatever made up her past and present.

"They have amazing scones," Ember said. "My treat."

That evidently sealed the deal. K stepped into the room. But instead of letting the door shut, she turned and whispered something. A small, hooded figure slipped around the corner of the doorframe where she'd been out of sight. A couple inches shorter than K, she tucked against K's side and grabbed her hand. Together they walked toward Skyy.

Finally, the front door closed with a bump, cutting off the frigid air. The central heater struggled to regain control of the room. The other patrons were probably relieved, but no one said a word as the girls stopped in front of Skyy.

"This is Olivia," K said. "She needs your help."

Inwardly, Skyy's heart broke. It was difficult to determine Olivia's age with only her face showing, but she was younger than K, who couldn't have been over fifteen. They *both* needed help, but K wasn't ready to admit that for herself—at least not in front of strangers.

"Hi, Olivia," Ember said. "Want something to eat?" She held her hand out to the girl. Olivia cut a glance to K for approval before letting go. She followed Ember, but skirted the offered hand.

Trust was—and would be—an issue for both these girls, and Skyy couldn't blame them. She turned back to K. "How about you?" She hitched her chin toward the bar.

K started forward just as the front door burst open triggering the jangling bells. She spun and lost her balance in the oversize shoes. Skyy wrapped her arms around the girl to keep them upright as they both stared at the teen couple who had entered.

"Sorry!" the female of the couple said, laughing.

"It's starting to snow!" the boy said.

A rattle of chairs filled the room as everyone still sitting got to their feet and hurried to the front windows. Skyy felt K relax, then stiffen again as she realized Skyy was holding her. Skyy loosened her grip, allowing the girl to stand on her own, but Skyy kept her hand on K's arm.

"It's okay. You're safe here."

K straightened and took a breath.

"You know my name," Skyy said. "Will you tell me yours? Unless *K* is your real name."

The girl shook her head, but hesitated. Skyy could almost hear the wheels turning as K evaluated the situation, the people—most especially Skyy.

"It's Bailey," she said at last. "Like Baileys Irish Cream, except without the *s*. My dad thought it was cool. That's what my mom told me."

Even though Skyy hurt for the girl, she couldn't help but grin. "I guess that makes us two of a kind. I'm named after vodka; you're named after Irish whiskey. We'll be unstoppable!"

It was stupid, she knew, but she was grasping at anything to build rapport with this girl.

Olivia and Ember came by on their way to the front windows, and Ember handed Bailey a huge chunk of scone. Bailey took a tentative bite, then closed her eyes and let out a small groan.

Skyy laughed. "That was my reaction too." She turned the girl toward the front windows. "So, where did the *K* come from? Is that your middle initial or something?"

Bailey shook her head. "K-A-Y. Kay was a girl I knew last year. She died."

Skyy shuddered at the raw statement as Bailey went to the window and inserted herself between Ember and Olivia. Was that to preserve her role as primary in Olivia's life? A mother or big sister figure?

"Well," Connie whispered, coming beside Skyy and leaning close to her ear. "*This* is interesting."

The lump in Skyy's throat kept her from speaking, but she nodded.

"Where are they from?"

She shook her head. "Maybe Ember knows."

"What are you going to do?" he asked.

This was so far beyond her knowledge and experience. She thought Ember would be challenge enough, but she was eighteen and technically on her own. Sure, she'd been in some lousy foster homes—as well as some good ones—but she'd never had to survive on the streets. What did that do to young girls? Were they damaged for life? Beyond help to ever be normal?

She shook her head again. So many questions, to none of

which she had answers. Asking her mother certainly wasn't an option, and she had no aunts or close girlfriends.

"Call the police, or FBI, or...somebody."

She needed help, and only one name was forefront in her mind.

Canon Truax.

Would he know what to do? Maybe at least know where to begin. Meanwhile, these girls needed a safe, warm place to stay. And real food. Had either ever eaten a salad?

Connie rested a hand on her shoulder. "I think they need *you* tonight," he said so only she could hear, "but I can make some calls tomorrow—if you want me to."

She glanced at him as he moved away and mouthed *thank you*. They'd met only a short time ago, but he was already a friend willing to help.

Beyond the store windows, darkness had fallen, hastened by the heavy skies. Exterior building lights and signs illuminated white flakes slanting sideways as the storm continued to blow through. Now that the rain had softened to snow, a few brave souls left their shelter and stood in the middle of the street with faces turned up and tongues extended to catch the frozen treats.

The three girls stood shoulder to shoulder along the front windows. Ember was the tallest, followed by Bailey, and then petite Olivia. Except for Ember's darker coloring, the three could pass as sisters.

But one thing for sure, Skyy Delaney wasn't their mother. Neither was Skyy D.

CHAPTER 22

After a marathon with prosecutors on Sunday, testifying in the San Diego court Monday, and returning for grueling cross-examination by defense attorneys today, Canon wanted nothing but to get to his apartment in L.A. and crash for several hours. Driving back to the cabin tomorrow would be soon enough.

At the advisement of the prosecutors, he'd worn his sling for the sympathy vote. It hadn't helped at the hearing, and his shoulder ached more than it had while doing light work at the cabin.

And eating would be good. The sadistic attorneys for the perps somehow convinced the presiding judge to continue straight through the lunch hour, arguing that every minute their innocent clients were in jail was an infringement on their civil rights. Canon had never heard of that happening, and it confirmed the DEA's suspicion that the cartel had influence over the judge. Breakfast of seven hours ago had long since worn off.

He exited the courthouse into light steady rain. The same storm front assaulting the middle of the state had worked its way southward, coming ashore Sunday afternoon and bringing much needed moisture to the lower half of the state. It showed no sign of moving on.

Canon had to shake his head at last night's news. The weatherman opened the broadcast with the most important question: When will the rain end? Moisture was inconveniencing all the convertible drivers and golfers. San Diegans loved their sunshine.

While he walked north on Union Street to the parking lot, he powered on his phone. It dinged several times, indicating both text and voice messages. He half expected all to be from Captain Olenski, ordering him to report for duty. But then he saw the messages were from Skyy's phone.

The text messages were *Call me,* and *Call me now.* Time and date stamped from this morning while he'd been on the witness stand. The voicemail, also from mid-morning, was more interesting. He missed hearing her voice and was anxiously awaiting tonight's *Night Thoughts* show. He pressed the Play icon.

"Canon…uh, hi. Sorry we didn't get to talk before you left. I have a question for you. I mean, I have a situation…sort of."

She paused and sighed.

"Actually, it's too complicated to explain in a message because I'm sure you'll have questions." Her voice dropped as if she were speaking to herself. *"A lot of questions."*

He pressed the phone tighter to his ear as a loud truck roared past on the street.

"Could you just call me as soon as you receive this?" Another sigh. *"Thanks. Bye."*

The message ended, and Canon lowered the phone and stared at it, as if doing so could decipher the meaning behind her words.

He pressed the Call Back link as he neared the entrance to

the parking lot, pausing as the call rang. Skyy's voice message came on.

Someone slammed into his back, knocking his right side forward. Pain shot through his shoulder and arm like an electric current. He staggered, spinning fully around as he fell to protect his injured shoulder. The sidewalk was as hard as he expected it would be, but he shielded his injured arm by landing on his left side.

Two teens were sprinting away, laughing. One held Canon's cell phone high. That would stop the minute they discovered the phone was a piece of junk about ready to die.

A portly man—probably a defense attorney if the expensive suit he wore was any indication of his profession—helped Canon to his feet. But then he hurried away, not even bothering to ask if he was all right. Yep, defense attorney for sure.

Canon leaned against a light pole, taking deep breaths while waiting for the pain to subside. Then he headed for his truck where he'd left the meds.

He could buy another phone, even a cheap burner temporarily, but Skyy's number was programmed into his old one, and he didn't have it memorized.

He unlocked his truck and climbed in, debating his course of action. It was still early enough in the afternoon to beat much of the traffic out of San Diego, but by the time he got to Los Angeles… Well, there was *never* a good time to be on L.A. freeways, so it didn't matter much.

He wanted to get home back to the lake.

And talk with Skyy D in person.

"Hi, all. Skyy D here, and you're listening to *Night Thoughts* on Black Owl Radio. I hope you're having a good evening. Thanks for dropping in for my ramblings and to hear some great music from independent artists all over the world.

"Good to be back with you after surviving that virus. Man, that was nasty stuff. A special thanks to my friend, Ember, for being my voice when mine was AWOL. If you enjoyed hearing her, send me a post. I'm pretty sure I can persuade her to step back in periodically." Skyy grinned at Ember, who rolled her eyes.

They were sitting at the counter in DC Coffee long after hours. The front blinds were closed, and the only light came from two fixtures near the front windows, the counter lights behind the bar, the back storeroom, and Skyy's laptop. She nodded at Ember to click the next song, signaling Big Jerry to start it playing.

"This is Wayward Bunny's new release, 'Grass Cutter,'" Skyy said over the song intro. "Enjoy." Ember clicked the microphone mute button.

Skyy glanced over to check on Bailey and Olivia, who were sitting at a table a few feet away. Enough light came from the back room so they could read magazines and books available from the shop's free exchange shelf. The girls had asked to stay at the cabin, but Skyy insisted they come along. No way was she leaving them to their own devices. Plus, she still hadn't talked to Canon. His number came up on her phone hours ago, but the call dropped and he hadn't left a message. When she called back, it went straight to voicemail. If he came home tonight as planned, finding two strange girls in his home wouldn't be good.

She rubbed at the tension between her eyes. Even if she intercepted him, she had no idea how she would explain Bailey and Olivia's presence. He was a cop. How would he handle having two tight-lipped underage girls—possibly runaways or worse—sleeping on his floor and eating his food? Labeling it presumption on her part didn't even begin to cut it.

She should have asked Connie about who he might call, but last night had blindsided her. Getting the girls home, bathed, dressed in some of Ember's clothes, fed, and bedded down with spare blankets had sapped every ounce of her energy.

And today, when she tried to question the girls with all the tact and sensitivity she could muster, they deflected her attempts like seasoned manipulators. Her inquiry about parents led to *what's for lunch*? Asking about where they lived brought a suggestion they all go for a walk. When she broached the topic of anyone looking for them, they pummeled her with questions about the size of the lake, if they could swim in the summer, if she ever ate a fish caught there, and could they all go camping in the teardrop in Yosemite? Canon was a trained interrogator—that's what she needed with this pair.

One bit of information she managed to wring out of the girls was their ages. Bailey was sixteen, and Olivia was fourteen. At least that's what they said. Who knew? In normal clothes they looked more like thirteen and ten.

She stared at the girls happily reading, as if being up past midnight in a closed coffee shop was a normal experience. Skyy shuddered, realizing maybe this was the *best* experience they'd had this time of night in a long while.

In a distant corner of her consciousness, she realized Ember was speaking.

"...'Finding Clover,' by Color The Wall. Let us know what you think of their music. When we come back, we'll be talking about safety tips for Spring Break." Ember clicked the mute button. Big Jerry swelled the music as she turned to Skyy.

"Sorry," Skyy said with a weak smile. "I don't even know why I'm here."

Ember dismissed that with a wave of her hand. "You're here because you're the star."

"I feel more like a fizzled comet."

"Just remember," Ember said, "it's you that Canon tunes in to hear. Wherever he is, he's probably listening right now."

Strangely, Ember's words were a comfort. Even a one-way connection to Canon was, well, a connection. Still, it was beyond bizarre that their conversations so far had been limited to posts and messages through Black Owl, one very public phone call, texts, and her voicemail message. Yet she was living in his house!

Despite their communication shortfalls, she had the photos. She knew his face, the line of his jaw, the distant look in his eyes. Yeah, and the abs.

She smiled. Tomorrow she would meet him and talk face to face.

Canon blinked at a pair of oncoming headlights, concentrating on keeping in his lane while making sure the other car stayed in *its* lane. San Marcos Pass wound through the mountains between Santa Barbara and Los Olivos, shaving ten to fifteen minutes off the main Highway 101 route through Gaviota.

In the daytime, The Pass, as everyone called it, provided gorgeous views of the ocean, mountains, majestic oaks, and Lake Cachuma. At night, however, the mostly two-lane highway was notorious for cars hitting deer, running off the steep road, and some tragic head-on crashes. Add the pouring rain coming down now and it had him wishing he'd opted for the longer, safer route. Still, he wanted to get to the lake as soon as he could and find out about Skyy's "*situation*."

He'd bought a convenience store disposable phone and called the cabin. From the fast busy signal he heard, the lines were still down. Then he called Mart—the only other phone number he had memorized—and asked if he had numbers for anyone else in Deer Cove. He didn't, but volunteered to look up some numbers—as soon as his team mopped up an apartment complex fire. Could be a while. Canon could have called information for DC Coffee, but he didn't want to stop.

He slowed as his headlights lit up rocks washed down from the steep hillside on his right. Unable to go around the obstacles in good conscience, he stopped, turned on his emergency flashers, and then stepped out into the wet. Even a road worker rain suit wouldn't have kept him dry as he bent over the first of two basketball-sized rocks. Rolling it with one hand took serious effort, but he cleared both boulders before too many vehicles lined up behind his truck.

Water ran from his hat and clothes when he climbed back in, soaking the upholstery and fogging the windows. He shifted into gear and started forward, but had to slam on his breaks as a Corvette whipped around the cars behind him and cut in front of his truck, narrowly avoiding an oncoming van. Canon checked his side mirror before accelerating again.

Skyy would be finished with the *Night Thoughts* show by now. If he'd been able to listen in, he could have phoned the call line and gotten a message to her. He sighed, vowing to memorize more phone numbers, especially hers.

Twenty minutes later, he reached the junction where he merged back onto 101 North. He rolled his neck, working at the kinks and groaning at the soreness. His formerly good left shoulder took the brunt of his fall in San Diego, so now he was crippled on both sides. Tomorrow was going to be awesome.

But first, he had at least two more hours on the road. In the dark. In the rain.

Regardless, in a few hours he would talk with Skyy D in person.

CHAPTER 23

Skyy kicked aside the blanket and an annoying dream in one motion. Nightmare, really. She'd been sleeping deeply, then had one of those endlessly frustrating episodes about the first day of school and not being able to locate her locker. Never her problem back then, so why stress over it now in a dream?

After using the bathroom, she tiptoed down the dark hall to get coffee started. She avoided the clock. That it was still before dawn was knowledge enough. She usually slept late after a show night, physically and sometimes emotionally depleted after an hour fielding comments, questions, and occasional callers. Not this morning. It depended on the topic, of course. Love topics were the easiest because no one knew anything about how it worked—especially her.

She paused at the living room, distracted by the two girls piled in blankets sleeping in front of the flickering fireplace. Whatever last night's discussion had been, today would be like one giant *Night Thoughts* dealing with the toughest questions on the planet. For that she needed much caffeine.

The under-cabinet lights glowed way too bright, and she squinted as she filled the coffeemaker and pressed start.

While it took its sweet time heating and gurgling, Skyy sat at a barstool and rested her head on crossed arms.

Whether Connie came through with some help or not, Skyy would have to call someone in authority. Was it a crime to keep these two girls without telling someone? Probably. Her being hauled off to jail certainly wouldn't help. What if they asked for a permanent address? *Homeless* wasn't the answer she wanted to give.

If only Canon would call—but he couldn't because she didn't have any cell service here and the house phone was still dead. She lifted the handset just to make sure. Yep, dead. Since he hadn't come home last night, he'd probably be here for sure sometime today. This morning, maybe. She rubbed her face, anticipating the conversation.

"Well, Canon, see I was trying to help this girl who called and, well, it sort of turned into two *girls."*

Yeah, no. She'd have to do better than that.

A chunk of wood shifted in the fireplace, sending a burst of sparks against the glass. In the momentary light, she realized there were three bundled forms, not two. She stood and walked closer. Olivia was the middle form, flanked on one side by Bailey and the other side by Ember. She had probably gotten up to add wood to the fireplace and decided to join them. Again, Skyy had the image of three sisters, Ember being the older responsible one.

Skyy shook her head and slumped back to the stool. Sisterhood and one big happy family wouldn't be happening here. Daylight would bring harsh reality, cruel and indifferent to the wants of Bailey and Olivia. Ember knew that better than most, which was probably why she was sleeping on the hard floor rather than in the bedroom. Time was precious.

Skyy wiped her eyes, then poured the finished coffee into a large mug and headed toward the back of the house. The girls had piled their wet clothing on the washer last night. If this day was going to suck, she might as well start it off with laundry. Any day, no matter how bad, improved after laundry.

Her plan was to close the door to keep the light and noise from waking the girls, but as Skyy walked into the laundry room, she tripped over something and sprawled flat out on a lumpy form. When the form moved, her scream woke everyone like no light or chugging washer ever could.

"Skyy. *Skyy!*" Canon wrapped his left arm around her as she flailed on top of him. If she didn't stop soon, things were going to get embarrassing. "It's me, Canon." She finally slowed her struggles and pushed her palms against his chest to create some space. *Ouch.*

"Canon?" she said. "What are you doing here?"

He grinned, even though she couldn't see him in the dark. "Uh… I *live* here?"

She slapped his chest. *Ouch.* "Yes, but what are you doing *here*?"

"Well," he said, doing his best to ignore the length of her body, her heat seeping through his sleeping bag, "I got in really late, and all the beds and floor space were taken."

The hallway light flashed on, sending a harsh rectangle of light across their length. Skyy twisted to look, and Canon raised his head so he could see over her shoulder. Ember and two younger girls crowded the doorway, blinking with sleep.

"Skyy?" Ember said. "What happ—holy crap." She put her hand over her mouth.

"Language," Skyy said automatically.

"Is that your dad?" the youngest girl asked Ember.

The middle girl nodded. "Probably."

Ember gave up trying to hide her grin, and Canon started chuckling. Skyy glared at him and swatted his chest again. *Ouch*.

"You better take your hand off my butt, Truax," she growled in a whisper, "or I'll have you arrested."

He slid his hand up to her lower back—slowly—failing to keep a straight face as she slow-boiled.

"It's not funny," she snarled.

"Yeah," he nodded, "it sorta is."

"Yep," Ember chimed in.

The small girl asked, "Why is your dad sleeping on the floor?"

Canon laughed out loud, as did Ember.

"What?" asked the girl innocently, looking between the other girl and Ember in turn.

Skyy lowered her forehead to his chest, and soon her whole body began shaking too. "Crap," she mumbled.

"Language," he whispered in her ear. She shook harder.

"It's still night," the older of the two strange girls said, yawning. "I'm going back to bed."

"Me too," said the younger one. They disappeared down the hall.

Ember leaned her shoulder against the doorframe. "I'm staying."

"Go to bed, Ember," Skyy ordered, her voice muffled against his chest.

"Yes, ma'am." She straightened and left, but not before flashing Canon a grin and exaggerated two thumbs up.

The hall light went out, leaving the laundry room in darkness. They remained motionless for a minute.

"This is nice," he said, moving his hand in small circles on her back. Skyy began shaking again.

"Except…" he said, "am I wet?"

"Coffee," she said.

"Not right now, thanks."

"No," she said, levering off him. "I spilled my coffee when I tripped over your big feet. Good thing the sleeping bag insulated you because it was scorching hot." She got to her knees and opened the dryer door so they could see by its interior light.

"Looks like you got it too." He pointed to the brown stain covering the front of her T-shirt.

"I guess we need to shower," she said, plucking the wet cloth away from her skin.

"I'm up for that." He shoved the wet bag down to his waist and sat up.

"I didn't mean…" Her cheeks turned red and she jumped to her feet and backed toward the doorway. "I mean…" She turned and fled.

"Save some hot water for me!" he called, then started laughing again.

This was a lot more fun than listening to her on the Internet.

CHAPTER 24

SKYY HELPED CANON HAUL A CHIMINEA TO THE EDGE OF THE front porch. He laid a fire in it, stoking it with all the wood that would fit while she moved the two chaise lounges closer. But despite the nearly red-glowing earthenware, she shivered when the breeze raced down the planks and hit the side of her face. With the girls inside, she and Canon needed privacy so they could talk, but she wished they'd camped out in her teardrop with the portable heater.

Canon brought out another blanket and wrapped it around her from behind, draping it over her head like a shawl. It was hot, fresh out of the dryer, and she sighed as the heat soaked in.

"Thanks." She smiled up at him. He wore a heavy coat, gloves, and a ski hat pulled low over his ears. "I can't believe it's still this cold. I thought the sun would warm things up."

"In a few months we'll have days over a hundred, and you'll be wishing for this."

A few months. Would she even be here then?

She stared out at the lake, gray and unfriendly under some thin clouds. Last night's brief snowstorm, if you could call it that, hadn't lasted more than two hours, dusting trees, roofs, and roads with a thin layer of white that made the drive home a little slippery. Except for a tiny patch hidden in the shadow at the base of one of the bigger pines, it was only a memory.

Canon wedged two more sticks into the chiminea. "Are you hungry? Thirsty?"

"It's only 11:00."

"Be right back," he said, disappearing inside.

He returned a few minutes later carrying a plate with a three-inch-tall sandwich of turkey, lettuce, tomato, and cheese. And two cans of orange soda, one of which he passed to her. But instead of sitting down and digging into the food, he put it on the side table and stood beside her.

"What?" she said, stopping her move to open the soda. "Aren't you going to sit?" Instead of doing so, he pulled the glove off his left hand.

"We haven't formally met." He stuck out his hand and smiled. "Canon Truax, police officer, part-time resident of Storm Lake."

She reached toward him automatically, then jerked her bare hand back before they touched. "Sorry. Skyy Delaney, possibly still contagious. Uh…squatter at Storm Lake."

He grinned at her and tossed the glove onto the small table. "I guess those are kind of long for everyday names. You can call me Cop Hottie for short, like Ember does."

She burst out laughing, covering her mouth, then her eyes, with both hands. When she dared look, Canon grinned even wider as he settled on his chaise.

The man had grown out of his boyish good looks present in some of the online photos, images she had virtually memorized. She blamed that on Ember. But because of Ember's interrogation abilities, Skyy knew Canon was twenty-nine years old like her, never married and not in a relationship, had a brother named Martin, and lived full time in Los Angeles but was working in San Diego. He'd been a cop for seven years.

And—as Ember also said—Canon Truax could be the model for a recruitment poster. *Cop Hottie Wants You*. Whew. Where did she sign up?

But it was his eyes that drew her in until everything else about his face faded. Unlike so many guys, he wasn't looking over her shoulder or checking his phone. His gaze stayed centered on her, interested.

Skyy realized they'd been staring at each other way too long, and it was getting awkward. They popped the tabs of their sodas at the same time.

He took a long drink. "I hope the store in town has more of these. Actually, I'm not sure why I bought them. I haven't had one in years."

She glanced sideways at him, stilling her own can at her lips. "Orange sodas have always been my favorite."

He raised an eyebrow, then smiled as if not surprised.

She shook her head. "I have to apologize."

"For...?" He bit into his sandwich and chewed, watching her.

"Showing up unannounced without an invitation, spreading germs all over your house, crashing your weekend getaway."

He swallowed the food. "First off, Ms. Possibly Contagious Squatter, I *did* invite you…in one of my posts to you on Black Owl. I said something like *if you ever need anything*. Second, Ember called and I told her to come." He turned back to his sandwich. "As for the germs, I'm finishing a course of post-surgery antibiotics. They probably aren't anything like the meds you're taking, but maybe they'll do some general good and keep me healthy."

"Still, this is more than a little…" She motioned between them.

"Awkward?" he provided, shifting slightly to face her. He grimaced as he tried to find a comfortable position, but he hid it under another grin. He was recently out of surgery and still in pain—not to mention her falling on him in the laundry room—yet he'd built a fire, brought her a warm blanket and a soda. Taken care of her.

"Definitely awkward," she agreed. But nice.

"So, the girls…" he began, holding out his plate so she could snag a few chips she'd been eyeing. "You seem to be collecting them. Any more on the way I should know about?"

"I hope not." For a cop, he was taking the situation rather well—or he was suffering from sleep deprivation from the long drive and scant rest. "No guarantees."

He nodded.

Skyy filled him in with what she knew. He'd heard Bailey's first call as K a couple of weeks ago and how it ended abruptly. She explained about the second call when Ember filled in, and how Ember gave out Skyy's phone number and their location. Then K—now known to be Bailey—arrived with Olivia in tow.

Canon had talked to the girls this morning while Skyy made breakfast, but they were tightlipped when it came to last names, details regarding parents or relatives, and addresses or phone numbers. Maybe that was because they heard Ember talking about him being a cop. Of course, things couldn't remain like this forever, but Skyy suspected that's exactly what Bailey hoped would happen. Calling the teen skittish would be an understatement, but Skyy saw the beginning signs of relaxing. Perhaps a couple more days would bring out their stories.

One clue to the situation they came from was when the

house phone rang an hour ago. Both girls startled, and Bailey jumped to her feet. It was only Ember calling from DC Auto to report the phone lines were fixed. Deer Cove was back in touch with the outside world, good or bad. Evidently Bailey interpreted it as bad.

"At some point we'll have to inform Child Protective Services," Canon said, staring into the crackling fireplace.

"I know," she said. "It's just... It sounds so institutional." She lowered her voice, though the girls were inside where it was warm. "If they were caught up in some sex trafficking prostitution ring..." She pinched her eyes shut against the image.

Canon scooted to the end of the chaise and crammed gnarled oak branches into the chiminea. Fragrant smoke swirled around the L-shaped porch.

"Sorry," she said, clutching the blanket tighter. "Life isn't fair on so many levels. I just wish there was another way besides giving them to overworked, understaffed authorities."

Canon was silent for a few minutes, then cleared his throat. "I know a woman. AJ Stone." He pointed left along the shore of the lake. "She and her husband, Alex, own some cabins over there at Bass Point. They rent them out, primarily to fishermen. Their place isn't far, but the road doesn't go through."

Skyy remembered her trip out on the ATV and running into the road-closed signs.

"Did you ever hear of the shooting at Desperation Falls?" Canon asked. "Close to four years ago now."

Skyy shook her head, not sure where he was going with the change of topic. "I wasn't anywhere near here then."

"It made national news too," Canon said, leaning forward

and holding his gloved hands toward the fire. "Too complicated to go into all of it now, but the basics are that a psycho held a girl hostage down south. Murdered some people. The girl escaped and ended up here when she was fifteen, I think. She stayed with AJ. Alex was here, too, but this was before they got married. It all ended when the psycho tracked her here to the lake."

Skyy leaned forward, dreading the worst. "What happened?"

Canon smiled. "Let's just say that AJ Stone is someone you want on your good side. As is Alex, who is former DEA. Teal is their adopted daughter."

Skyy breathed again. "Teal's the girl? She's okay?"

He nodded. "I've met her several times. She's more than okay. Amazing, really. Brilliant. You want *her* on your side, too. But my point is, AJ took Teal in when she was only fifteen and a runaway from foster care. And AJ wasn't about to let the authorities put Teal back into that same system. Maybe she can help in our situation."

Our situation. Skyy's body sagged with relief. Instead of being mad about the estrogen invasion of his home, Canon was willing to help. That simple word *our* shifted everything from her shoulders alone to a partnership, and that was comforting.

He surprised her further by reaching over and taking her hand. Although his was gloved again, the gesture warmed her as much as the fire. After all, what was a layer of leather between them when earlier this morning she'd been sprawled on top of him, lips close enough to kiss. And why, in the middle of this crisis, was she thinking about kissing Canon Truax? She shook herself.

"Can we call this AJ woman right now? Or drive to her place?" She pushed her chair back and stood. "I don't want to wait another minute." He rose and snaked his good arm around her back. She stumbled against him.

"Relax. I called her before I came out with your blanket. AJ and Teal will be here in—" Gravel crunched around the side of the house and they turned toward the sound. "I suspect that's them."

Skyy took a deep breath. While it irritated her that Canon called this woman without discussing it first, she was relieved it wasn't all on her to figure out the next step.

From what Canon said, it sounded like Teal ran from the system. Would Bailey bolt when she found out others were getting involved? She had reached out to Skyy. Would she trust anyone else? So many questions.

She glanced at the cabin window. Both the girls were on their knees on the sofa, faces to the window. Bailey had a cell phone up like she was taking a photo. When they saw Skyy looking, they disappeared. Great. Skyy had a sneaking suspicion Ember would receive a text with a photo of Skyy and Canon hugging.

"Hi, Canon," said a tall blond woman stepping onto the porch. "And you must be Skyy. I'm Lena Stone, but most people call me AJ. Good to meet you."

Skyy returned the greeting. The slight pressure of Canon's hand at her back reminded her to relax and breathe.

A girl appeared from behind AJ. She had short black hair, dark eyes, and an infectious grin.

"Skyy D," the girl said, stepping forward and grasping Skyy's hand. "I'm Teal, and I listen to every *Night Thoughts* show. This is so exciting! I can't believe you're right here at Storm Lake!"

Skyy flicked Canon a glance, one he returned with a one-shoulder shrug that said, *I might have let it slip when I called.*

"And living right next door!"

Teal squealing like a fangirl was the last thing Skyy expected. True, the girl didn't do quite that, but she did almost dance on her toes. Canon's hand increased pressure on Skyy's back as he leaned close to her ear.

"Looks like you have another dedicated listener. Besides me."

"Is Ember here too?" Teal said, peering around Canon at the front windows. "I *love* her."

Canon laughed, and Skyy elbowed him in the ribs.

"Ouch."

"Sorry." But it served him right.

"I like them," Skyy said to Canon as they waved goodbye to AJ and Teal.

He nodded. "It's a tight community. Good people who can depend on one another."

AJ had laid out a ton of information about becoming a foster mom, sharing her experience going through the process so Teal could stay with her. It had been a scary time, because there was no guarantee it would work out that way.

However, becoming a foster mom was not on Skyy's radar. She just wanted to protect the girls. Her family had been the poster models of dysfunction, and surely that disqualified her from even *thinking* in that direction. If she wanted to, which she didn't. Obtain some help for Bailey and Olivia? Sure, absolutely. Those girls deserved so much more than what she suspected they fled from. But that didn't mean she was the one to provide a home—if she had one to begin with, which she didn't.

Skyy sighed inwardly. It seemed there were a lot of things

she didn't want to do. Had she taken time to ask what she *did* want?

Life was coming at her faster than she could handle. The weight of her responsibility with Ember was heavy enough, but at least their relationship was more mentor and mentee, with Skyy providing a safe fallback as the teenager grew into self-sufficiency. Skyy knew first-hand how to do that. But a foster mom? No way.

Still, when she looked at those two girls…

She shivered, recalling Teal's story of bouncing through several homes, running away, living on the streets, being kidnapped, escaping, nearly dying, then being hunted again by the same sick predator. Would that be the fate of Bailey and Olivia if they didn't have a stable, safe environment?

Teal still bore visible scars—she'd removed her jacket and showed Skyy some of them. The emotional damage cut deeper still, and raised its head mostly as paranoia, which Teal said she embraced as *"useful in moderation."*

What invisible scars did Bailey and Olivia have that would surface in a month or in a year?

"I don't even know where to begin," she said.

"My dad always said to begin with the basics," Canon said, "and I guess the most basic thing is that the girls are here, warm, and safe."

"And that they can't stay—at least not legally or for long." Not without Skyy getting into legal hot water. She wasn't sure what that would be, but hiring a defense lawyer wasn't in her budget. She rubbed her forehead, wishing she were somewhere else—like a deserted island in the Pacific with white sand beaches a whole lot warmer than here.

Maybe a cabana boy to serve colorful umbrella drinks and play soothing guitar music under a nearby palm tree—so not *totally* deserted. She closed her eyes, picturing the lapping waves, swaying palms, the cabana boy…who looked exactly like Canon Truax. When she opened her eyes, Canon was staring at her with suspicion.

"So," she said, giving herself a mental shake clearing away the white sand, "do you know this sheriff AJ mentioned?" Sheriff Derrek Cabot had been the one who vouched for AJ in her bid to keep Teal.

"I've met him," Canon said. "He brings his family to many of the events here at the lake. July 4th fireworks, the fall festival—that sort of thing. Seems like a straight shooter, by-the-book guy. Although from what AJ said, it sounds like he has a soft side."

She hoped that was true. The information Teal garnered from the girls was enough to leave Skyy relieved in one way and scared in a whole new direction.

CHAPTER 25

"WHY ARE YOU SENDING THEM AWAY?" BAILEY SAID LATER THAT afternoon, as she and Skyy watched Canon, Ember, and Olivia drive off in his truck. They were getting ice cream and drinks at DC Coffee, then picking up a few things at the grocery store.

Skyy studied the girl. From what Bailey told Teal, the girls hadn't been part of a sex traffic ring per se, but they *were* part of a cult-like group that dangled young girls as bait to entice willing customers who *thought* they were buying sex. The group leader—a man known as Gabriel—enlisted several burly group members who posed as undercover cops complete with fake badges.

It was a simple con. The girl or girls dressed provocatively and had flowers in buckets when they engaged the customer at his car window. Then the phony cops would step from the shadows at the last minute and "convince" the customers they really *did* want to buy flowers from the girls—at a steep price. Some just stomped on the gas and split, but others were willing to shell out fifty bucks for a few roses to avoid arrest. The ruse netted Gabriel a fat profit.

Teal had believed the story, but Skyy suspected there was

more to it, and that Gabriel wasn't an altruistic provider for those needing a place to live. Could be the way Skyy's skin itched when Teal mentioned his name.

"*You* called *me*," Skyy said. That first phone call had been a cry for help. "And now I think it's time you tell me some things."

She led them back inside and they sat by the fire. A dozen questions demanded answers. Bailey glared at her for a moment, then turned to the dancing flames. A long few minutes of silence passed.

Skyy sighed. "Let's start with your story. Your parents?"

The girl got up and went into the kitchen. For a minute, Skyy thought their conversation had ended before it began. But Bailey returned with two cans of orange soda, handed one to Skyy, and sank cross-legged onto the carpet. They popped the tops in unison and sipped.

"I never knew my dad," Bailey finally said. "One time, I think it was in third grade, we were supposed to write about our families. Mom said I didn't have a father. Said to never ask her again. End of story."

"What did you do?"

"I made up some BS about his being in the army and dying in Iraq when I was a baby—how all the aunts and uncles and cousins cried at his funeral." She shrugged. "Who knows? Maybe it's true. Or maybe he's out there somewhere, wondering about me."

That last held a thread of hope and wistfulness that resonated with Skyy. Maybe every kid fantasized about having a happy family who loved and cared for each other.

"So...what about your mom?"

"She didn't pick me up after school one day." Bailey set her can down on the brick hearth, forgotten, same as she had been that day. Same as she still was.

Skyy leaned forward as Bailey recounted going to a temporary foster care home that night and a new school the next day. Weeks passed while her caseworker tried to locate her mother and relatives. Then came three more homes and corresponding new schools before finally identifying a cousin in Oakland who said he'd take her in.

"So, you have aunts and uncles?" Maybe there were other extended family members who could help.

Bailey sipped, then shook her head. "Not that I ever heard about—other than the ones I made up in that story."

"But this cousin…"

"He was a forty-year-old single guy who had the same last name as me: Miller. He promised my caseworker we were family. I don't know for sure, but I bet she called everyone in the Bay Area with that name. I never met him until the day she dropped me off at his house."

"Okay," Skyy said. "I take it things didn't work out?"

Bailey laughed. "Oh, they worked out great—for cousin Jimmy." She did air quotes around 'cousin.' "That was his name. My stay with him lasted just long enough to finish the paperwork and close my file. I mean, how screwed up is a system that turns over a young girl to an old single guy with no proof he's even related?"

A system that was overwhelmed by families blown apart by drugs, crime, and hate. And too many government leaders who were more concerned about posing with sexy photo op projects than actually helping those in need. A few billion for an overpriced bridge or a train to nowhere? No problem. But a fraction of a percent of that money for more child welfare resources? Sorry, just can't afford it.

"A few weeks later, this man named Gabriel came by the house to visit my cousin—who, of course, wasn't my cousin at all. I heard him tell Gabriel that." Bailey shrugged again, her go-to gesture. "He seemed nice enough—better than Jimmy. And he had a cute little black dog named Maxie who had soft, curly fur and a white spot above his left eye."

Skyy raised a brow.

Bailey rolled her eyes. "I know, I know. *'Hey, little girl. Want a piece of candy?'* But I was only ten." She grabbed her can and drank.

"He said he'd take me to a McDonald's that had one of those fenced play areas and I could order anything I wanted, even a sundae. Since Cousin Jimmy's idea of dinner was a six-pack, Gabriel's offer sounded great. He loaded my stuff into his car, then gave Jimmy a fat envelope. We stopped at the McDonald's like he promised. I fell asleep after that and woke up when we turned into a long driveway somewhere in the country."

"Was it just you then?"

Bailey shook her head. "There were three older girls, a boy, three women, and four men. We had a few goats, tons of chickens, and a giant garden."

"Sounds like a commune. Was it a big house?"

"The main house had five bedrooms, and there were four cabins and a barn. We also had over a hundred rose bushes. That's how that whole selling flowers gig started." Bailey laid on her back and laced her fingers behind her head, staring at the ceiling, remembering.

"Every night after dinner, we met for what Gabriel called *Awareness*. He'd talk about all sorts of things: caring for the earth, politics, finances, the evils of pesticides, our souls. I couldn't understand most of it. But he always said how God talked to him in his dreams and told him what to say and do."

"And everyone believed him?" Skyy said, trying to keep the incredulousness out of her voice.

"I guess." She turned toward Skyy. "I mean…they all did what he said. Even me."

Yeah, but you were a child. "So, you were there for what, five or six years?"

Bailey nodded.

"And it wasn't too bad?"

Bailey stared at the ceiling. Her lips tightened and her jaw muscle clinched. Sky would have missed it if not watching closely.

"Something changed," Skyy said.

Bailey picked at a piece of lint on the carpet. "When the girls turned eighteen, we had birthday parties for them. Then they were separated from us younger ones—moved to a building hidden in some trees across this deep canyon that cut through the property. It had beds, a kitchen, and guards. That's what they told us. We weren't allowed to go there, and the girls never came back to visit. Gabriel said they were adults now and needed their privacy."

"Did you believe him?"

"I snuck out one night last fall after everyone was asleep. The moon was nearly full, so I could see well enough. There wasn't any path down into the canyon I could find, so I climbed over fallen trees and fought through brush. A small stream ran at the bottom, but I used rocks as steppingstones. It was just as hard getting up the other side.

"It wasn't as nice as the big house. There were dead shrubs out front, and half the porch railing was on the ground. I remember hoping the inside was fixed up."

"Did you go inside?" Skyy asked.

Bailey shook her head. "It was hot that night and one of the side windows was shoved up a foot. I tiptoed around and peeked in.

"A small lamp was on, and I saw a girl named Amine

sitting on the side of a single bed. She'd turned eighteen two months before and disappeared from our group. Her head was down in her hands like she had a headache or something, but I knew it was her by the red hair. I whispered her name, and she looked up."

Bailey was silent for a minute, and Skyy wondered if she would continue.

"I don't know who was more startled. She didn't expect to see me, and I expected to see the girl I knew before. But she didn't look the same." Bailey slowly shook her head. "Not at all. Both her eyes were bruised black, and her lower lip had a gash. She looked like she'd been in a car accident or something. Mostly what I remember about her was the blankness in her eyes."

Bailey barked a single laugh, but there was a sadness that weighted the sound, like it would fall back from the ceiling and crash around them. Skyy shifted on the couch, uncomfortable from sitting so long, but more so at what she dreaded was coming.

"That's when Amine told me about the other side of Gabriel's business. No more selling flowers. Our 'guards' forced Amine and the others to go with the customers. Amine fit Gabriel's business perfectly. He wanted the girls to be eighteen but look younger." She turned a wry smile toward Skyy. "A man with scruples, I guess. Anyway, Amine filled me in on what would happen to me when I turned eighteen."

"Is that when you called me?" Skyy asked.

"Yeah, that first time," Bailey said, sitting up and hugging her knees. "I listened to your show whenever I could, but Gabriel kept us so busy I missed a lot of them. And I didn't always have a phone. That night was rainy and cold. No one was out on the streets. My guards went to get coffee, and I was able to listen. I was planning to run away but had to skim some money first. Things were going pretty well for a while, and I thought I had a little time."

"What happened?"

"A couple of weeks ago, Gabriel drove up to our compound in his gold SUV, and Olivia got out of the backseat." Bailey turned and looked at Skyy. "She was playing with Maxie."

Another recruit…lured by the cute dog. Another girl who would find plentiful food, a safe place to live. Another girl who would grow to trust Gabriel, but who also faced Amine's future—and Bailey's. Skyy swallowed hard to keep her stomach stable. Picturing Gabriel strung up by his round parts helped.

"I couldn't let it happen to Olivia," Bailey said, fierceness in her tone.

Neither could Skyy. She wasn't sure what she could do, but no way was she letting these girls go back. Not even if they all had to flee cross country and live in the teardrop.

She knelt beside the girl and wrapped her arms around her. "I'm sorry," she said into the girl's hair. "I'm so sorry."

CHAPTER 26

Skyy was finishing the never-ending dishes when a Ford Explorer with a sheriff's department door emblem turned down the driveway and stopped outside the kitchen window. She dried her hands and made it onto the front porch as a uniformed man ascended the side steps. Bad timing had Canon at a doctor visit in Mission Peak. Ember had taken the girls to work with her at DC Auto to help organize the owner's chaotic filing system and parts catalogs. Skyy was on her own.

"Good morning," he said, removing the flat-brimmed trooper's hat he'd just settled on his head. "I'm Sheriff Derrek Cabot."

"Skyy Delaney," she said, stepping forward and extending her hand. It was a move to establish some control—she'd learned that from a book about body language and interpersonal contact. However, as a woman she couldn't come off as too aggressive. Men, especially those in uniform, didn't like that. She gave his hand just the right pressure.

When he held her hand a few seconds longer than she expected and gave her a small smile, Skyy knew she'd lost the advantage. Maybe he'd read the same book. This man might be sheriff in a mostly rural county, but he wasn't a pushover.

She invited him inside and offered coffee, which he accepted. Then they moved to the dining area.

"Beautiful flowers," the sheriff said as he took a seat opposite her.

Heat reddened Skyy's cheeks as she shifted the bouquet Canon brought her from somewhere in town. She wasn't sure what to make of the man who had rapidly become such an integral part of her life. Only a couple of weeks ago he'd been a fantasy photo on her computer. Now—

"I spoke with AJ Stone," the sheriff said. "She speaks highly of you."

"Really?" The word was out before she could grab it back, before he raised both eyebrows. "I mean…well, we just met. We don't really know each other."

Derrek Cabot smiled at her. "Her husband, Alex Stone, is former DEA. Still has friends in the right places that owe him favors—if you know what I mean."

"He checked me out?" Knowing her life had been sifted through by law enforcement was more than a little unnerving, but at least the sheriff hadn't arrived brandishing handcuffs.

Cabot chuckled. "On the other hand, if I had something to hide, I'd worry more about that daughter of theirs."

"Teal?"

"She's like a walking lie detector and computer hacker all in one. She can ferret out more in thirty minutes than my men and women can in a week." He sipped his coffee. "She's something, all right. I may have to hire her."

"So…" Skyy said, "I guess you didn't come to arrest me?" She meant it as a joke, a continuation of breaking the ice. He shook his head but returned only the barest smile.

As if God tracked the man's mood, a cloud obscured the sun and transformed the cozy eating area into an interrogation room. A shiver crawled up her spine.

Sheriff Cabot steepled his fingers and leaned across the table.

"Tell me all you know, Miss Delaney."

Skyy collapsed on the sofa as soon as Cabot's SUV turned out of the driveway. He'd filled a notebook with dates and details, and now—after Skyy called Ember to make arrangements—he was meeting the three girls at DC Coffee to garner more details.

She tried to give him money to buy the lunch for the girls, but he wouldn't hear of it, promising to take care of it himself. His changing moods made it difficult to predict the man. Useful in his occupation, she supposed, but it gave her a bit of emotional whiplash. Before leaving, he asked if Bailey or Olivia had been in touch with anyone since arriving.

"Not that I know of," she said, realizing she should have had Bailey promise not to contact anyone the second they burst into DC Coffee Friday night.

Skyy shivered at the meaning behind the question, even as sunshine once again flooded the cabin, the rays doing their best to warm her. At least the day was warming, and the air leaking in the open kitchen window was fresh and sweet, suffused with wet pine, damp earth, and spring's promise of new life.

Her stomach growled, but she couldn't eat knowing Sheriff Cabot would soon be with the girls. Even though Bailey and Olivia fled from Gabriel, they'd probably been taught to mistrust the police. Would they clam up the second they spotted his uniform? Or worse, disappear at their first opportunity.

She rose and paced the living room, the space suddenly too small. Until a few days ago, her life had been solely in her own hands. Loser Boyfriend's leaving had forced her to take charge. While scary at first, she had grown confident on her own, comfortable. Then Ember arrived, then Canon, now Bailey and Olivia, and suddenly she was doing breakfast dishes as everyone else took off for the day. An apron and doing laundry would come next, and that was *way* too domestic to contemplate.

She needed to get out. Except for a few puffy white clouds, the skies this morning were bright and clear. And the ATV was back under the carport and topped off with gas. She had to get back to planning life instead of accepting whatever came at her.

Staying with Canon wasn't a long-term solution. Although she could pay rent, his brother was half-owner of the cabin and might want to use it. And if she was going to stay at Storm Lake and explore a relationship with Canon, she needed to find a place of her own. Not that he was in any way like Loser Boyfriend, but she'd learned that lesson. A little distance meant safety—of her heart, at least.

The air was cool and breezy outside, but Skyy's layers topped by a sweatshirt easily kept her warm as she checked the ATV and wheeled it to the middle of the carport. She banded her hair in a ponytail and threaded it through the back of one of Canon's ball caps, then mounted the four-wheeler. She paused when Ember drove down the driveway, parked, and climbed out.

"The sheriff wanted to talk to the girls alone," Ember said. "Where are you going? Do you want to take the Jeep?"

Skyy shook her head. "You'll need it to bring the girls

home later. I just want to look around, get a feel for the town."

"Check out the Art Mill," Ember said. "Teal has some artwork there. I'm grabbing lunch here, then I'll go back and wait for the girls." She mounted the back step, then turned. "Oh, and I have a shift at DC Coffee from four to seven. I forgot to tell you. Are you home to watch the girls tonight? I can probably change if—"

"Ember," Skyy sighed, "it's not your responsibility to watch them. And thanks for taking them with you today."

"I know," she said, looking at the ground. "But they're here because I gave Bailey our location."

"No," Skyy said. "They're here because they needed to get out of a desperate situation. If not for you, Bailey would have found somewhere else." Or not. And that would have been the worst outcome of all.

Ember considered that for a moment, then said, "I'm glad they chose us." She opened the door and went inside.

Skyy started the ATV's engine, waiting a minute as it warmed up and smoothed out. "So am I, Ember. So am I."

CHAPTER 27

THE SHERIFF'S FORD WAS PARKED IN FRONT OF DC COFFEE WHEN Skyy made the turn onto Main Street. She felt a little guilty driving the non-street-legal four-wheeler on the road, especially past law enforcement, but there were two similar machines nosed into the curb in the next block, and there weren't that many cars around. Maybe off-season road rules were more lax than summer. Canon would know. He'd also know where to take Ember for her driver's license.

Skyy cruised by the storefronts, some of their names familiar from Ember's exploits: Peg's Waffle House, The Crab Shack, ViceCream, a chocolate shop, a bar called the Fish Hook, and Embers – Fine Dining.

She parked across the street from a white chapel that sat on a low, grassy mound overlooking a small marina. Sailboat masts swayed behind the structure, rendering the scene postcard worthy. A marquee sign announced Sunday service at 10:00 a.m. and had a number to call for booking weddings and special events. While she'd never been much for attending church in larger cities, it might be nice to see what this small community offered.

After wandering through a vintage clothing shop with

attached used bookstore, she inquired about the Art Mill. The woman behind the counter walked Skyy out the front door and pointed down the street.

"See that bridge over the main road? That's over Connor Creek that runs into the marina. Just this side of the creek and to the right, there's a small parking area. There are signs and a great path along the creek if you want to walk. Only a quarter mile or so. Or you can drive across the bridge and turn on Old Mill Road, but it's quite a bit longer."

Skyy thanked the woman. It took less than two minutes to fire up the ATV and drive the short distance to the graveled parking area. Only three cars occupied the fenced space that had room for a dozen. An oval Art Mill sign pointed up creek. She parked, pocketed the keys, and set off on foot along the path paralleling the rushing water.

The creek—actually more of a river after all the rain—tumbled over rocks as it rushed toward the marina and lake behind her, creating an enveloping roar that bounced off the majestic oaks and sycamores growing along the banks. It felt like she was in her own private, mystical forest, alive with buzzing insects, butterflies, birds, the stream, and every surface washed clean by the rain. She breathed in the smell of all things growing and lengthened her stride on the slight incline. While the desert around Tucson could provide cool, early morning hikes, it lacked the array of heady fragrances found here.

A second sign directed her left across the creek on a footbridge, and then along a path that led around the end of a huge log building she determined was the Art Mill. Several cars and a tour bus filled the parking lot. She climbed the broad steps onto the porch and went inside.

The high-ceilinged room was bustling with shoppers crowding around display cases of polished logs and glass.

Easels and shelves held paintings, ceramics, wood carvings, and pencil drawings. Cables suspended gnarled branches from the beamed ceiling, and each horizontal piece had rows of hooks for hanging necklaces, scarves, and small canvases. The opposite wall was mostly glass and overlooked an outside deck above the creek.

She was drawn to a large watercolor of a waterfall splashing into a pool festooned with leafy ferns, flowering plants, and moss-covered boulders. The colors were bright, giving an airy, positive energy to the painting.

"Skyy?"

She turned at her name and found Teal standing beside her.

"Do you like it?" Teal asked, smiling at the painting.

"It's stunning," Skyy breathed, leaning forward to read the small white placard. "*Desperation Falls: Salvation and Hope, by Teal Stone.*" Skyy jerked her eyes to the girl beside her. "You did this?"

Teal laughed. "It's one of the shoppers' favorites."

Skyy turned back to the painting. "I can see why."

"It comes in four sizes, and a wall mural is available online." Then she pointed to a display case nearly obscured by women. "And I have some miniature pendants that I make with Mina. She owns Palomino Glass Company, and also does these amazing glass sculptures."

"I'll have to meet her." Not that Skyy could afford any of the glass works Teal pointed out. Two were inch-thick glass sheets about four feet square with scalloped, broken edges. One had the image of a beautiful mermaid, the other an angel wrapped in her own wings. They were mounted in rectangular glass basins filled with colored clear marbles and strands of tiny seed lights.

"Mina lays out the image on the reverse side, sandblasts it, then airbrushes in the color. Everything is lit by LEDs."

The detail on the faces, mermaid scales, and angel feathers was so precise that from a few feet away they looked like photographs.

"You should see the full-size angel she has up at her house on the hill. And if you ever need anyone badass to protect you, Mina's your gal."

The strangeness of the statement drew Skyy's attention away from the sculptures. She expected to see a grin. Instead, Teal's expression was one of absolute seriousness. "I—"

"You or the girls," Teal interrupted. She paused a minute while two women passed by, then said, "Life isn't all pretty butterflies and mermaids."

Skyy didn't doubt it for a second, and if anyone knew from experience, it was Teal Stone.

When the sun hid behind thickening clouds and cast the interior of the Art Mill into shadow, Skyy figured she better not push her luck. She said goodbye to Teal and promised to come back the next day and meet Mina.

A brisk wind pushed her along the path, bending trees and sending leaves scuttling ahead. She jogged the last part to the ATV. A smattering of raindrops set her teeth chattering before she pulled even with DC Coffee. Stopping for a hot drink didn't even tempt her. As she passed Bibs' Beauty Barn, all she could think about was getting to the cabin, stoking the fireplace to white-hot, and huddling in front of it for a day or two.

She twisted the throttle and the little motor revved higher. The age-old question was, would speeding up and getting out of the rain sooner keep you drier than slowing down and being in the rain longer? But with the wind and dropping temps, quicker was definitely the better option. She gritted her teeth and clinched her knees against the machine as she sped up a little more. Why was it nature conspired against her every time she ventured out on the thing?

The single hairpin turn on the route appeared out of the mist. She braked, intending to make the sharp right and accelerate into the next straightaway. But the new rain had washed soil down the ravine, smearing a muddy slick across the pavement. The ATV's front tires lost grip as soon as they hit it. Skyy careened across into the left lane, the machine jerking wildly as the front tires once again found clean surface and the rear tires entered the muck.

The four-wheeler spun in a full circle, then slammed nose first into the drainage ditch on the far side of the road. Skyy catapulted over the handlebars, flipping upside down and landing on her back on the steep bank. Air burst from her lungs.

She slid headfirst into shallow water running in the bottom of the ditch. It soaked her hair and scalp, sending chills throughout her body. A knobby rubber tire pressed into her left cheek, and pungent exhaust fumes from the idling engine burned her nostrils.

After a few seconds of frantic panting to get her breath back, embarrassment overcame the shock of the accident and spurred her to move. She twisted sideways until she was lying fully in the ditch, feet pointing uphill. The water instantly soaked her entire right side before she struggled to her hands and knees, wheezing and coughing.

She rested for a moment, head hanging down while muddy water dripped from her hair. Each inhale brought sharp pain in the middle of her back. A glance at where she'd landed revealed a large boulder. That it was mostly buried in the muddy bank didn't make her spine hurt less.

She sucked in a breath, held it, and reached for the ATV for support. Sharp pain sent her back to all fours. This wasn't going to work. The sounds of an approaching vehicle caught her attention. As mortifying as this was, she needed help. Through her dripping hair, she made out the side of a pickup as it stopped behind the ATV. The emergency flashers pulsed as the door opened and booted feet stepped out.

"Skyy?"

Canon Truax.

Ninety minutes after the accident, Skyy stood under the hot shower spray, rinsing the last of the crusted mud from her hair. The wet heat eased the ache in her arms and back. But no amount of washing could cleanse the underlying embarrassment of needing Canon Truax to pull her out of the ditch.

Ignoring her wishes, Canon had driven her—muddy hair, clothes, and all—to the clinic in Deer Cove for X-rays. Doc Arnold pronounced her bruised but unbroken. He suggested ibuprofen, a hot shower, then ice packs—exactly what she'd told Truax.

Though irritated, she was grateful for his help. Ever since Loser Boyfriend deserted her, taking care of herself had been a necessity, and she'd grown comfortable with it. This dependency thing was nice in some ways, but itchy in others.

When the water began cooling, she turned it off, toweled herself dry, and wrapped a spare towel around her hair. She should dry it now, but raising her arms above her head sent spasms down her back. Maybe ice would sufficiently numb the bruised muscles so she could handle the hairdryer.

Her trusty sweats never felt so good as she made her way to the living room where Canon had a fire going.

"How are you feeling?" he said, coming from the kitchen and setting a cup of coffee on the end table.

She answered with a groan as she sank into the sofa. It took her minutes of careful maneuvering to get comfortable, time enough for Canon to return with ice packs wrapped in a beach towel.

"Lean forward," he said.

His warm hands skimmed along her body as he adjusted the bundle between her back and sofa, sending shivers up her neck and down her arms that had nothing to do with the cold packs.

"I can help you dry your hair later," he said, his breath whispering against her neck as he leaned close. "Between my one good arm and your bad back, we can probably get it done, although I don't claim to be an expert at styling."

He sank onto the sofa beside her, his warmth hotter than the wood stove. What was it about this man that he could produce chills and heat with a touch?

Her eyelids drooped, her body giving in to the adrenaline depletion after the accident. The soothing hot shower and warm fire sealed her fatigue. The crackling flames filled the otherwise quiet room, and she realized this was the first place she'd lived with a real wood-burning fireplace. Hissing gas logs didn't count. This was like another person in the room, breathing, moving, alive. Mesmerizing. Her eyes closed all the way.

"Why are you barefoot?" he asked, rousing her from near slumber.

"Couldn't bend over that far," she mumbled.

He rose, leaving a void of cold where he'd been, but returned seconds later and lifted her right foot. She felt his hand working a thick sock over her toes, around her heel, and brushing the bare skin of her ankles as he pulled it up her calf. His fingers lingered for a few seconds, then he tugged the sweatpants' elastic down over the sock. He repeated the procedure for her left foot, and she wished for the first time she was a four-footed animal. Or an octopus.

"How are you not married, Truax?" she said as he settled beside her once more. Instead of laughing, he pressed closer along her side.

"Never met the right girl before."

Although in near stupor, she was alert enough to process the *before* word slithering across her consciousness.

Ember would be jumping and cheering if she heard Cop Hottie utter it.

CHAPTER 28

"ARE YOU SURE ABOUT THIS, CANON?" EMBER GRIPPED THE steering wheel of his truck that he'd just turned over to her. He'd taken her place in the passenger seat. Although he tried to be stealthy, she saw him tighten his seatbelt.

"It's the best way to get completely comfortable," Canon said. "Not much harder than Xbox."

That got her smiling. Skyy had evidently shared that tidbit about her driver training. And it wasn't like she hadn't driven through that storm with Skyy practically unconscious. Still, pushing the limits was something else.

They were at the far edge of an empty parking lot in front of what was once a grocery store in nearby Blue Rock Harbor. A row of orange cones stretched down the length of the blacktop. She flexed her fingers, working out the stiffness.

"Now," he said, "just take it slow at first. We'll build up speed as you go."

Ember pressed the gas and steered around the right side of a cone, then crossed the centerline and rounded the left side of the next one. After four or five, she began to get the hang of the right-left-right movement, and her steering became more fluid. Then she swung too wide around one and clipped the next cone when she under corrected. It thumped underneath the truck.

"Whoops."

"Straighten out and keep going," Canon ordered when she lifted off the gas. "Faster. Left, right, left, right…like skiing a slalom course. Look where you're going, not at the cones." He leaned his body left and right, matching words to motion and getting her to follow his lead.

She focused on the bushes at the end of the track, *feeling* the truck round each cone rather than looking directly at them.

"Good," he said when she stopped at the far end. "Better than a lot of police candidates do on their first runs."

"Really?" She took a few deep breaths.

"Yep. They're too cocky, always trying to beat each other. That's fine for some things, but driving is about concentration and controlled movements. The faster you go, the smaller the movements." He pointed down the line. "Drive back so I can reset that downed cone and you can try again."

And she did. After ten runs, he had her practice accelerating from a standing stop, flying down the parking lot and slamming on the brakes when she reached a pair of cones. The tires squealed, and the pedal pulsed under her foot.

"That felt weird," she said.

"It's the Anti-lock Braking System. If a car is equipped with ABS, no matter how hard you stand on the pedal, the system turns the brakes on and off several times a second to keep the wheel from locking up and skidding. Really great in the rain. Practicing teaches you what it feels like to go beyond normal. Most drivers never try this except in an emergency, then they freak out."

After an hour, and before darkness fell completely, he had

her backing up in a straight line, backing in left-hand then right-hand full circles, then doing the cone line again backwards while looking out the rear window and driving with only her left hand. That was super hard, and she knocked down nine of the cones. When fully dark, he had her make forward slalom runs with her headlights on.

"Good job, Ember," he said after they loaded the last of the cones into the truck bed. "I pronounce you ready for your driving test. After you pass the written one, of course."

"Thanks," she said, climbing back into the passenger seat for the trip home. "I've practically memorized that dumb book. Did you know there are almost more rules in it about graffiti, when you can and can't drive, and driving siblings or friends, than how to actually drive?"

Canon laughed. "Yeah, I've read it. But you'll do fine on both tests. You have good instincts."

His confidence in her was a new thing in her life—except for Skyy, who was always encouraging when she wasn't sounding like a mom. Even the occasional mom voice was okay, just different from what she was used to.

"You'll be a good dad." The words slipped out before she thought to stop them. "Sorry, I—"

"You think so?" he said.

"Sure." She couldn't leave it there. "I mean, dads have to teach their kids stuff, like driving. You're pretty good at this."

"Thanks," he said, his voice quiet. His face was lit up by an approaching car's headlights.

"Was it hard when your parents died?" she asked.

He nodded and took a deep breath. "It was. Still is. Mart and I weren't ready for that at all." He glanced at her, then back at the road. "But I guess you know a little about it."

"Yeah, well, my dad wasn't ever there, so I didn't really lose him. And Mom …"

"Parents are important. They aren't always the best at it, but most of them try hard."

"Skyy will make a good mom. You can do a lot worse, you know."

He laughed and looked over. "That your idea of a subtle hint?"

It was her turn to laugh. "Just sayin'. And I don't think I have to set you up."

He shook his head but said nothing.

They drove toward Storm Lake in comfortable silence. But her mind was anything but quiet. She'd been thinking a lot about family since her eighteenth birthday, and even more since she met Skyy. Both her and Skyy's parents had majorly screwed up, yet Skyy had turned out okay, and Ember thought she was doing pretty good too.

Mrs. Oso always told them they didn't have to repeat the same mistakes their parents made. Ember believed that. Everyone made their own decisions, good or bad. She wanted to make good ones. But life wasn't easy, especially when she was on her own. And with Skyy alone too, she sort of hoped they could be like a family.

"What if kids could sort of pick their own parents?"

It wasn't until Canon laughed that she realized she'd said it out loud. He smiled at her. It wasn't a dismissive smile like he thought it was a dumb question. More like he was thinking about it.

But now with Bailey and Olivia here—and Canon—Ember's relationship with Skyy was a lot more complicated. Before, it was only the two of them on the road. Now there were like a dozen choices instead of just one simple one.

She put her head back against the headrest and flexed her fingers.

"My driving with one hand making you nervous?" Canon

asked, nodding to her hands. His lips teased another smile, but his eyes were serious.

She shook her head, staring at the road ahead. Dark twists and turns. Until you got there, you didn't know what was around the corner. She'd read something similar in one of the V.M. Narrano books Connie had lying around at DC Coffee.

Life is full of choices. Make one. If it doesn't work out, make a better one.

That's what she needed to do.

"That was a pretty deep sigh," Canon said. "Anything I can help with?"

Ember sat up straighter. "I just made a decision."

He glanced at her. "A good one, I trust."

She crossed her fingers and sent up a prayer.

She sincerely hoped it was a good one—both the prayer and the decision.

"Got it!" Ember said, grinning as she came out of the Mission Peak Motor Vehicles building the next day, waiving her driver's permit. She leaned into the Cherokee. "Ninety-eight percent. Want me to drive?"

"Go for it," Skyy said. Her back was still sore from the ATV crash, so she couldn't win an argument about who was the better driver when she could barely look over her shoulder. They switched seats.

Ember started the engine and pulled out of the parking lot. She handled the Jeep with ease, checking her mirrors regularly, and even heeding Skyy's caution about not following a slow-moving van too closely. Of course, she'd had a lot of illegal driving practice before taking the written test, including the harrowing night they arrived at Canon's cabin. Skyy had no doubt the girl would pass the actual road test with a high score too.

"Mark's got an old Suzuki Samurai at the garage that someone gave him as payment for fixing another car," Ember said. "He said he'd sell it to me cheap if I help him reassemble the engine that the previous owner tore apart."

An unsettled lump formed in Skyy's stomach. "Aren't those the ones with a reputation for rollovers?"

"Yeah," Ember said, "but it has a roll bar."

"Oh goody. I feel *sooo* much better."

Ember laughed off the criticism as she flipped on her blinker and changed lanes. "Samurais got a bad rap because idiots drove them like sports cars. I won't be doing that. It's red and cute, and the soft top comes off, which will be awesome for around the lake in summer, don't you think? And it's four-wheel drive—in case of bad weather."

"Like another snow at Storm Lake?"

Ember grinned. "It could happen."

"Sure, in twenty years."

"We'll have to stick around and see," Ember said, sending Skyy a pointed look.

Skyy turned to the side window, watching the buildings give way to green hills as they headed up Highway 1. Everywhere else she'd lived after Loser Boyfriend had been short term, several months at most. She told herself it was exciting to see new places and experience new things. But maybe being constantly on the move was a guard against being disappointed—either by a place or by a relationship.

In Ember, Skyy had found a friend, and Ember thought she found a stable adult. Skyy laughed at that absurdity.

"What?" Ember asked, glancing sideways. "You think I'm

making a bad move with the Samurai?"

Skyy shook her head. "Just thinking." But not about the car purchase. Ember had said *we'll* have to stick around. As in them together. And since Ember made no secret she planned to stay in Deer Cove for a long time, she was laying the *stay* question all on Skyy.

It was evident in how the girl inserted herself into the community, bringing home news about new people every day. Her front desk presence at DC Auto had already increased Mark's business. People would stop by to talk with Mark, and before they left, Ember had scheduled an oil change, tire rotation, or other maintenance for their cars or trucks. Mark was already talking about bringing on a part-time mechanic.

But it was her job as a barista at DC Coffee that quickly connected her in depth. Connie Langworth told Skyy that Ember excelled as a marketer. Nothing that she consciously did, she just *was*. People came into the shop to talk to her.

As a natural introvert, Skyy could barely conceive of working such a job. Give her a microphone and an anonymous presence and she could do battle throughout the ether world. But face-to-face with people all day? Nope. So not happening.

Perhaps that's why she enjoyed the peacefulness of the rolling hills, the rocky Pacific coast, the beautiful lake. This place felt comfortable.

And Canon Truax, a man who could be fun and spontaneous—she'd seen the pictures—could sit beside her for an hour without saying a word. Could she imagine a life at Storm Lake with a cop?

"Canon?" Ember asked.

Skyy turned. "What about him?"

"You're smiling," Ember said, grinning herself. "I figure you're fantasizing about our landlord."

"I wasn't fantasizing. Not exactly." She sighed. "Okay, maybe a little."

Ember laughed.

Skyy's smile faded. "I don't know what I'm supposed to do. I mean, there are the girls, finding a place to live, and Canon. Even you," she said. Then hurriedly added, "Sorry, that came out all wrong. I didn't mean—"

"Hey," Ember said, cutting her off. "I get it. A lot's been dumped on you, starting with me."

"No, that's —"

"Just listen." Ember made the turn onto the road that led toward Storm Lake, then pulled over and stopped in a gravel area. She shifted into Park and set the brake. She stared straight ahead, taking a few deep breaths.

"Ember, what's wrong?"

She gripped the steering wheel hard enough her knuckles began turning white. "From the moment I met you, I knew you were different. Truthfully, I sort of dumped *myself* into your life."

"Ember, I didn't mind."

"I know. But you didn't have much choice. Now, I've got something else to ask you."

"Anything," Skyy encouraged. She'd do anything she could for the girl after that blunder.

"It's kind of a big deal. Huge."

"Ember…"

"You're going to think I'm nuts, especially after what you just said about all the pressure and decisions and...all." She lowered the window and fanned herself with the cool coastal air. "But I've been thinking about this a lot."

"Is it something with the girls? If they're too much, I can—"

"I want you to adopt me," Ember blurted out.

"*What?*"

"Sorry, sorry. I mean I'd like you to *think* about adopting me. I mean, now that I've got my permit and will soon get my license and have a car, I won't be a burden to you or anything. I promise."

As stunned as Skyy was, she managed, "You're not a burden. Never."

Tears welled in Ember's eyes, and her breath came in jagged cycles.

"Since I'm eighteen and legally an adult, it's a pretty easy process. Adoption, I mean." She stared out the windshield. "I'll save up money to pay the attorney fee, and it only takes a couple of months at most."

A couple of months? The girl had researched this.

Ember turned, chin trembling, eyes downward. She swiped the wetness away. "I know we're not exactly the ideal mother-daughter combo. I'm too old, and you're too young. But even if I get married someday to a great guy, I don't want to not have other family in the world." She looked up, her eyes glistening. "You don't have to be my *mom* mom and take care of me, but I want us to be a family. You and me."

Skyy's tears were flowing now, too, but she made sure her mouth wasn't open in shock. Ember hadn't known Skyy for long. That this young woman trusted enough to even ask such a question…

Ember wiped her eyes again. "When I have kids, you can be their grandmother." She grabbed a napkin from the door pocket and blew her nose. "But only if you want to."

Now Skyy's mouth *was* hanging open.

Ember took a huge breath and blew it out, then pulled the Jeep back onto the road and accelerated. "So… What do you say?"

Grandmother? She was only twenty-nine years old!

CHAPTER 29

"SO," CANON SAID, "WOULD YOU BE GRANDMA, GRAMS, OR nana?"

"Stop it!" Skyy said, throwing a dish towel at him, scowling when he caught it easily.

Every few minutes he'd break out with more chuckles or at least a wide grin that bordered on an irritating smirk. He didn't even try to hide it.

She'd sent Ember, Bailey, and Olivia to The Crab Shack for dinner, then to ViceCream for dessert. She planned some alone time with Canon after he got back from a physical therapy appointment. What she *hadn't* planned on was him finding her predicament so hilarious.

"Yuck it up, lawman."

"Sorry," he said, pretending—and epically failing—to wipe off his grin with the towel. He laughed again while mumbling "sorry."

"Yeah, yeah," she said, brushing past him and moving to the front window by the dining table. It was already dark out. The long days of summer couldn't arrive soon enough.

"Are you going to start doing your hair in a bun?"

She didn't take the bait, instead watched the lights from

homes across the lake in Shelter Cove. Families there were probably finishing their dinners. *Normal* families. Well, maybe not normal, but at least more traditional than the conglomeration in this house. She sighed, feeling his approach before noticing his reflection in the darkened glass. It was weird how she could sense his nearness even when he didn't make a sound.

"For what it's worth," he said, joining her in her window stare, "I think you'd make a great mom. You're kind, giving, and you have good instincts about what's right and wrong. You're a great role model." She was just about to thank him when he leaned close to her ear and whispered, "And you'd be the hottest granny at the lake."

She stepped away, facing him with crossed arms. "I didn't tell you the rest. When we came into the house, Ember was sounding out how *Delaney* worked as her new last name. Bailey and Olivia overheard. Now they want me to adopt them too."

His lips twitched, but he had the good sense to keep them closed.

"Then Bailey and Olivia argued whether *Truax* was a cooler last name than *Delaney*. It took them less than five minutes to have you and me married and adopting all of them. Three kids; you and me; cozy cabin by the lake. Do you think we should get a dog, *Daddy*?"

She turned back to the window. If only the darkness out there held wisdom that tomorrow's sunrise would reveal.

A log snapped in the wood stove, showering the glass door with sparks. Besides the hum of the refrigerator, it was the only sound. Canon remained silent, no doubt as stunned as she was by the whole situation.

Serves him right. But it hurt a little he wasn't immediately rising to her defense.

"Those kids are smart," he said quietly.

"Excuse me?" She turned to look at him. He'd settled onto one of the dining chairs, but his eyes were on hers.

"I mean, that's pretty creative. And when you think about it, it's not a bad idea."

"Truax, if this is your idea of a marriage proposal, it's the worst one I've ever heard."

"You've had a lot?"

"A few," she said, then clamped her lips tight. Okay, that was a stretch. But her college drama class play *had* run for two weekends, and each night the lead actor proposed to her character. So that technically made four marriage proposals. Sort of.

He stared at her for a full minute, all humor gone from his face.

"What are you thinking, Truax?"

He cleared his throat, looked out the window, then back at her.

"Would you say no?"

She sucked in a breath. It wasn't a proposal exactly, but it was close to the edge. Like a low rock wall at the rim of the Grand Canyon, one misstep and you were in for an unstoppable plunge. Probably why her stomach was in free fall.

She concentrated on not hyperventilating while she studied his eyes, his face, his hands clenched so tight his knuckles were white. The cop was nervous?

He hadn't asked if she would say *yes*, to which her automatic response would have been *no*. Instead, he'd flipped it and asked the opposite: if she would say *no*. That twisted it all around and required wrestling with the consequences of a negative answer.

A *no* response was a rejection of the girls' fantastical

scenario, and they might take that as a rejection of them personally. Not true, of course, but still… How would Bailey and Olivia feel if Skyy said yes to adopting Ember, but no to them?

As she studied the man before her, she realized he was waiting to see if she would reject *him* out of hand too. Or give him a chance.

Did he want a chance with her? Was he seriously considering the girls' cockamamie idea? Serious enough he would marry a virtual stranger to grant their wish for a family?

"Skyy?"

She put her hands over her face, blocking the sight of him while her body spiraled into an internal tornado.

In Tucson, she had things under control. Two streams of income, a decent car, a place to live. Now she had a would-be daughter, two more wannabes, and a guy sort of asking—even if it was the lamest proposal of the century—if she'd marry him so they could all be one big happy family. How did her life blow off the rails in only a few weeks?

"This isn't a Disney movie, Truax."

Chair legs scraped, and Canon's arm circled her back. She let him pull her into his chest. Though she kept her eyes closed, her arms went around him, and she rested her cheek against his hard muscles. The scent of his body wash soothed her as they swayed to silent music. In only a few days, he'd become a supportive friend, an ally in life. Maybe more.

Is that what she wanted? More with Canon? They'd had little time together, but he was the one she thought of when every question popped up, the one person she wanted to talk to, laugh with. Even when she was mad at him and he couldn't keep that playful smirk off his face, she missed him the second they were apart.

And when he talked about summer at the lake—the festivals, swimming, boating, early morning coffee on Connie's patio overlooking the water—she saw herself in every frame of that flickering movie playing in her head. The thought of moving somewhere else, of not being with him, getting to know him... That wasn't part of any future she imagined.

But was it even possible to figure out a relationship with everything else going on? They hadn't even begun dealing with the girls' emotional damage that was surely present under the surface. What guy would willingly take that on?

"This isn't going away, is it?" she said.

"Ember, the girls, or me?" he asked.

Any. All.

"Not Ember," she said. "I haven't told her yet, but I'm definitely going ahead with the adoption." Skyy pulled away from him and moved back to the kitchen to make coffee. Not that she wanted it. But ten more seconds of slow dancing and she'd be kissing him. By the fire. In a cabin by the lake.

Not that it would be so bad. He was probably as great at kissing as he was at everything else. The guy seemed as good as those first pictures promised. Ember was convinced. But Skyy's dependence on others hadn't worked out well in the past. She needed to be careful not to swoon just because the guy had abs to die for.

Canon took a seat on one of the bar stools, waiting—another thing he was good at. She poured water into the coffee maker, filled the filter with grounds, and pushed start. Only then did she face him, keeping the bar between them.

"I don't talk about it much, but my growing up life was a mess. Actually, it was normal at first, then my parents detonated our family by getting into drugs." She waved her hand at the memory. "Or maybe they were always into them and I never knew. I was young, so I don't remember them as adults, just my parents, you know? They could have been hiding all sorts of things for a long time."

He nodded. But how could he know? His family, from what she'd gleaned mostly from Ember, was happy right until his parents died.

"But then everything blew up," she said. "Mom and Dad were arrested for selling and put in jail. I was eleven, Vance was twelve." She got two mugs from the cupboard and set them on the counter. "We went to live with an aunt and uncle we barely knew. I think I'd met them twice, once when I was a baby."

She leaned on the counter for support, the memories heavy on her shoulders and heart.

"School was a struggle. I saw everyone having normal families except for me. It wasn't true, but it *felt* true." The few birthday parties she attended were most often at homes with both a mom and a dad.

"Vance had it rough too. But then he got into drugs at the beginning of his junior year. Life at our new home became like our old one—only worse." So much worse.

"My uncle kicked Vance out the day he turned eighteen."

"That must have been tough for you," Canon said.

She shook her head. "By that time, we were all worn out by his behavior. We knew several of the local police officers by name. So his leaving brought a sense of relief, as perverted as that sounds." She took a breath, tamping down the angry tears that still threatened.

"What was tough was seeing my brother do exactly the thing that destroyed our family in the first place. Nothing I said or did made an impact on him."

"You weren't his parent, Skyy," Canon said. "It wasn't your job."

"My job or not, I couldn't help him." She poured the finished coffee into the mugs. "My point is this: with Ember, I don't have to be a real mom to her. On paper, yes, but really I'd be more like an older sister. I can do that. She's quite independent, if you haven't noticed."

He smiled.

"But with Bailey and Olivia… I mean, I…"

"I get it," he said, accepting the cup she slid across to him. "You don't think you qualify as a mother."

"No, it's not that," she said, then recognized her defensiveness for what it was. "Well, maybe it is. It's not like I had a good role model, is it? But I don't see how I can ever adopt the girls no matter what. It's all the other stuff. We don't even know Olivia's background. She could have parents somewhere searching for her. And surely child services and the courts will place them in better situations than I could ever provide. They aren't going to turn them over to an Internet DJ whose home is an aluminum can on wheels."

Canon slid off the bar stool and walked into the living room. At first, she thought he'd grown tired of her whining, but then he returned with three thin books and began paging through them, looking for something. She recognized them as V.M. Narrano books, same as Connie had lying around DC Coffee. The author was a national sensation, made even more mysterious because he, or she, remained completely anonymous.

"Ah, here it is," he said, flattening one book open. "Listen to this. '*We don't choose our destiny any more than we design it. Our role is to embrace it when it slaps us in the face.*'"

"Destiny? So, I'm just supposed to accept any outlandish thing that comes my way?"

"Life is messy," he said.

She stared at him. His words made it sound like things could be fixed by running the vacuum cleaner or mopping the floors. "I think this is more like nuclear bomb messy."

"You're not alone, Skyy. I'm not going anywhere."

She turned her back so he wouldn't see the tears wetting her lashes, know how much she longed for that to be true. But how could she be sure? She'd failed with Loser Boyfriend. If that happened with Canon…

And none of his words addressed the most fundamental problem: she had no experience whatsoever in being a mom or foster mom. And although she knew it wasn't true, she still felt the sting of not being able to save Vance.

Skyy's proudest accomplishment was being a survivor. She'd done okay so far. But one minor crisis could bring even that crashing down, whether the disaster was a financial one or a busted relationship with her cop landlord—who had made his way around the bar and was rubbing her back and burying his nose in her hair at the moment. She leaned back into his strength.

"You're an amazing woman, Skyy Delaney, and I think you can handle anything life slings at you."

Including a cop she depended on more each day? Not that Canon was pressuring her or anything, but she'd learned a hard lesson when Loser Boyfriend's desertion had forced her out of her apartment. Canon lived in L.A. What would happen when he went back there?

Sorry, Narrano, but in her opinion, destiny sucked.

She wiped her eyes and stepped away from Canon, instantly missing his solid confidence. Oh, for something like this to be permanent. But just because she wanted something, didn't mean she could have it. Relationships were a crapshoot —all risk and no guarantees.

"What's wrong?" he said, reaching toward her.

Skyy held up a palm as she fumbled for an excuse. "It's eight o'clock, and I haven't even started to get ready for my show." It was lame, but the best she had.

He nodded, his face resigned. "Okay." He looked around the room, then at the black windows. "I think I'll get some exercise. Go for a walk down to the end of the road."

"But it's dark out," she said, stating the obvious. Had he already grown weary of her moody negativity? She knew she was sending mixed signals, accepting his embrace one moment, then pushing away seconds later. But so much of their conversation was still hanging without decisions.

"I have a flashlight." He smiled, but it was tinged with sadness. At least that's the way she interpreted it. "I won't be gone long. Go ahead and take the truck. The keys are on the hook by the back door."

A minute later, the door opened and closed, leaving Skyy alone with her problems in a house suddenly too empty and too quiet. She wanted to run after him, hold him. Have him hold *her*. Instead, there in the silence, his earlier question screamed at her:

Would you say no?

He'd left the book on the bar. *On Life,* by V.M. Narrano. The thing couldn't be eighty pages long. Was life so simple it fit on those few pages?

She sighed, tucking the book into her computer bag. Maybe there was something in Narrano's writings she could use for the show—slap somebody else with his destiny wisdom.

She changed into warmer clothes, grabbed the truck keys off the hook, and headed to the coffee shop where the Wi-Fi worked and she could hang out in the non-messy virtual world.

A few minutes later, Skyy was fitting the key into the lock at DC Coffee, when Ember, Bailey, and Olivia drove up and stopped. The Jeep's front passenger window whirred down.

"I got Maltese Falcon ice cream," Olivia yelled from the backseat, thrusting a dripping cone over Bailey's shoulder so Skyy could see.

"What about you, Bailey?" Skyy asked, walking to the passenger window of the idling Jeep.

"Cement Shoes." She held up a cup that held two grayish rectangles with small black boots imbedded on top. "Kind of like cookies and cream. And Ember got Pretty Boy Floyd. It's red, like blood."

"Sounds…yummy," Skyy said.

"We got some for you and Canon, too," Ember said, holding up an insulated paper bag. "We'll take it home and put it in the freezer. Unless you want it now."

Skyy shook her head. A sugar coma before a show wasn't a good idea, but she'd have something to look forward to. Maybe she and Canon could eat it later—together. "What flavor did you get us?"

"*Sex In The City*!" Olivia shouted, pumping her free arm in the air. "Woo-hoo!" Bailey laughed, shushing the younger girl. Clearly someone was already cresting a caloric high.

At Skyy's raised brow, Ember shrugged. "It's their newest flavor." The corner of her mouth turned up. "Guaranteed to please, the man said, so we got you guys triple scoops!" She stepped on the gas.

"Bye!" Olivia shouted as the Jeep sped away. Bailey trailed a hand out the window.

The Cherokee curved by the Swim Beach and then passed Bibs' Beauty Barn farther up the road. It was the most relaxed

Skyy had ever seen Olivia. Like three sisters out for an innocent, fun evening. God knew those girls deserved it. The taillights, a little blurry through her misty eyes, blinked out as the road climbed into the trees toward home.

Skyy remained on the sidewalk for a few moments. Other than muted thumping bass from the bar down the street, the loudest sound was ropes slapping against hollow sailboat masts as small wavelets entered the marina behind the shops. She breathed in the scent of oiled docks, fried fish from The Crab Shack, and pine. Come summer, families would grill hot dogs and hamburgers at the Swim Beach.

It wasn't hard to envision Ember, Bailey, and Olivia swimming in the roped off area or taking out a rowboat. What would it be like to live so close they could all load up ATVs and ride down to the beach? As a family.

She blinked away the Mayberry image. Scientists called it *idealistic distortion*. Reality, unfortunately, usually fell far short of dreams. Still, the happy hope persisted like a comforting blanket wrapped around her heart. Maybe Canon's optimism was warranted and something good could work out for them all.

"Sex in the City. Guaranteed to please." Skyy shook her head, laughing as she unlocked the door of DC Coffee. There was so much to be thankful for. Ember was such an amazing young woman. And, as crazy as it sounded, Skyy was suddenly eager to be her official mom. She'd tell her in the morning.

But first, Skyy might have a talk with ViceCream's owner about appropriate names for their desserts. Better yet, she could send in her personal Cop Hottie in uniform to convey the message.

Her phone rang as she locked the door behind her. Sheriff Cabot's name came up on the display.

CHAPTER 30

"HELLO, SHERIFF," SKYY SAID, BALANCING HER PHONE WHILE setting her equipment bag on the shop's counter.

"Sorry to call so late, Ms. Delaney, but I wanted to update you about what happened today."

An uncomfortable knot formed in Skyy's stomach, and she chose pacing rather than sitting as she listened.

"Over the last few days, I've been in touch with several Bay Area agencies. They helped track down this elusive Gabriel to an address in a rural area east of Oakland. The sheriff of Contra Costa County, James Willoughby, is an old friend of mine, and it turned out they were already investigating reports of suspicious activity. A lot of late-night comings and goings."

Skyy walked to the front windows and stared into the dark. She wished the sheriff would get to the point, but feared what she might hear when he did.

"With my information from Bailey and Olivia," Cabot said, "Sheriff Willoughby obtained a search warrant, and a joint task force raided the compound a few hours ago. They found two adults, three juvenile girls, and one juvenile boy who all appeared healthy. But they also found a cache of weapons, and one of the drug-sniffing dogs alerted to stacks of thousands of dollars. That was more than enough to close the place down and put the kids into protective custody."

"Did they find the other house?" Skyy asked. "The one Bailey said was across the ravine?"

"They did." Cabot cleared his throat. "I'm afraid it was worse than she recounted."

His description of the two girls in the house left Skyy shaking. He didn't have their names, but she hoped Bailey's friend, Amine, was one of the rescued girls. Heat rose as she realized again how close Bailey and Olivia came to ending up in that hellhole, beaten, frightened, forever scarred.

"And that bastard Gabriel… Did they lock him up?"

"Unfortunately, no," Cabot sighed. "He wasn't on the premises and hasn't yet been located. His real name is Bradley Farmer, thirty-eight years old. He grew up in the area, so he knows it well. Sheriff Willoughby issued a statewide BOLO. We'll get him, but there are over 100 cities and 7 million people in the Bay Area alone. It could take awhile."

Skyy cursed the man's name and didn't realize she'd spoken out loud until Cabot coughed.

"I do have some good news for you," he said. "In light of the Bay Area situation, our social services agreed to place your two girls in foster care with Alex and AJ Stone. They'll have to move to their property in the next couple of days. You can visit the girls whenever you like, and they can visit you. Mr. Truax being a cop carries some weight. Also, a preliminary search hasn't found any missing persons reports matching the girls' descriptions."

Your two girls.

Skyy latched onto that one ray of hope in Cabot's awful story. Now more than ever, that's the way she thought of them. With his call, it was like her protective instincts exploded inside, infusing every cell in her body with the overwhelming desire to care for them, keep them safe. And as nice as the Stones were, Skyy didn't want the girls moving to their property, next door or not. She wanted them with her.

CHAPTER 31

CANON RELAXED WITH THE FAMILIAR GREETING AND SEXY ALTO IN his earbuds.

"Hi, all. Skyy D here, and you're listening to *Night Thoughts* on Black Owl Radio. I hope you're having a good evening. Thanks for dropping in for my ramblings and to hear some great music from independent artists all over the world."

After bringing the ice cream—which Ember warned was for him and Skyy to eat *"together"*—she and the girls had showered, then left to join Skyy for the show. He had the house to himself. Just him and virtual Skyy D.

He was on one of the porch lounges, wrapped in two blankets against the night air, but Skyy's voice, rich and low, banished all thought of the cold. She credited her new microphone. More likely, he heard her differently because he wasn't distracted by her cute nose, gorgeous auburn hair, and those lips.

Out here in the dark with the stars twinkling and the full moon lifting over the hills, it was *only* her voice, and she was talking only to him. He closed his eyes and smiled, imagining

Mart howling at his sappiness. His brother could kiss off. Because Skyy D was living in his house.

"Later on, I'll be playing music by Wint, an amazing young singer you may have seen in her online videos. She's released her first full album, all self-written and performed, and she's only seventeen." Skyy laughed. "Makes me feel like a slacker, you know?

"At the close of Tuesday's show, Ember suggested a few topics for tonight. Thanks all of you who voted. The winning topic is risking and trusting in relationships. Those who have heard my story know I have some experience in this area, and evidently I'm not alone. According to a 2016 study out of Australia, half of people in long-term commitments don't fully trust their partner. They hold back, unwilling to risk everything. And 11 percent are convinced their partner would leave if he or she discovered one of those secrets. I think that's sad.

"But I'd love to hear what you think. So post a comment. Tell me how open you are in your relationship, or how open you plan to be in a future one. Do you fully trust your spouse or significant other?

"Meanwhile, starting off our music tonight is Positive Dream from Seattle. This is the third cut on their sophomore album, and it's titled 'I Want To Be Heard.' Appropriate, don't you think?"

Canon lowered his phone volume as the song played. The walk earlier had allowed him to reason through a few things. Skyy was scared, and it was no wonder. In a few short weeks, she'd gone from single woman to a houseful, and everyone wanting something major from her.

In the virtual world, he'd known her a lot longer than she'd known him. Months of listening to her voice—usually in the dark—gave him insights into what she cared about, what made her laugh, and how she treated callers. Truthfully, he'd fallen in love with her as a person. Not with her voice, but *her*. Weird, and perhaps he'd give Mart a nod at being sappy, but there it was.

On the other hand, she'd known him for only a short time, and most of that while holed up in this cabin with him and his bum shoulder. She'd never seen him whole, never had time to learn his opinions on tens of dozens of subjects like he had her.

His question earlier had dropped a bomb on her. He couldn't expect her to jump into his arms and commit to everything—whatever *everything* included. Ember's adoption, for sure. Skyy was determined to follow through with that. And hopefully *everything* included him, at least someday.

But the girls… Man, that was a huge responsibility, both for her and, if it went that way, for him too.

So being fair, he had to turn the question around and ask it of himself:

Would *he* say no?

Skyy had finished her intro and put on a Positive Dream song when a knock sounded on DC Coffee's front glass. Ember, Bailey, and Olivia stood outside on the sidewalk. Skyy rose and unlocked the door.

"I thought you guys would be getting ready for bed."

"We started to, but I wanted to be here with you," Ember said.

"And we wouldn't let her come alone," Bailey added.

Skyy pulled Bailey into a hug, then added Olivia. They smelled of shampoo, and Skyy pressed her eyes shut to keep from tearing up. She held the girls tight for several long beats until she felt Bailey squirm.

"What was that for?" Bailey asked as Skyy let them go.

"I just missed you guys," Skyy said, her voice ragged. "And…I'm glad you came back."

"Oh," Bailey said.

Olivia only nodded, covering a yawn. She pulled her hoodie up and slid into a chair at one of the tables, laying her head on her arms.

"Did you miss me too?" Ember asked, opening her arms wide, then added a whispered "*Mom*" when Skyy drew her close.

"Brat," Skyy whispered back, and Ember laughed.

Skyy surveyed the street before closing the door.

"Canon's on the front porch listening to the show," Ember said, answering the unspoken question. "Need help?" She hopped onto the bar stool next to Skyy's laptop. Bailey took one next to her.

"Under control for right now," Skyy said, catching the slight sag in Ember's shoulders. "But I'm not happy with the playlist. Why don't you reorder these songs while I hit the bathroom?"

Ember perked up and angled the laptop toward her and Bailey. Skyy looped around the bar and headed into the back room. The playlist was adequate as it was, but Ember would make it better. Skyy could walk right out the rear door and Ember would run the remainder of the show without a hitch. Her soon-to-be daughter was flat out amazing.

Skyy shut the bathroom door and splashed water on her face at the small sink. Truthfully, she was glad for the break. Sheriff Cabot's call had sent her emotions on an hour's long rollercoaster ride of horror, anger, and full-on fury. She'd barely pulled herself together in time to go on air.

She dried her face, used the toilet, and exited the tiny bathroom. On the way back to the bar, she stopped at Olivia's table and lightly stroked the girl's back as she slept peacefully. *May it always be so.*

She plastered on a smile and squeezed Bailey's shoulder as she took her seat by Ember. The mic was muted and a song by Wint was half done. "Did I miss anything?"

"Two more orphan girls called in and I gave them your address," Ember deadpanned.

"Very funny." Skyy bumped the girl's shoulder, and Bailey laughed.

Inside, Skyy was supremely glad Ember had made exactly that choice with an anonymous girl named *K,* who had shown up days later in this shop's doorway, half drowned with Olivia in tow. As much as any of the law enforcement personnel who raided that hellhole in Northern California, Ember was a rescuer at heart. So was Bailey. And Canon.

Maybe she was too. She wanted to be. If she would take the risk.

The song ended. Ember clicked the unmute button and Skyy leaned into the mic. "That was 'Bitter Question' by Wint. We'll have more from her in a few minutes, but first some of your comments. 21quido says 'Risk can be a quick decision, but trust is built over time.' Wise words, 21quido. You should write some lyrics for Wint.

"Desiringasgard notes that risk is never a sure thing but can be a calculated action. Man, you guys are deep tonight."

Ember tapped Skyy's shoulder and pointed to the mic. Skyy nodded and turned the mic toward the girl.

"Hi, this is Ember. I have a quote I found I'd like to read." She was holding a thin booklet, opened to its middle.

One of Narrano's books. Skyy hoped it wasn't more destiny wisdom.

"It's from *Love and Hurt,* by V.M. Narrano," Ember said. "You've probably heard of him; he's sort of a poet. Listen to this."

> *Those who refuse to risk miss true love. Deep, life-altering love can only be given, and we can't be the recipient without another first risking all. It's our choice to reject it.*
>
> *For anything given away risks not being returned. Our deepest desire is to love and be loved in a way that risks everything.*

"Isn't that amazing?" Ember sighed. "'*...to love and be loved in a way that risks everything.*' I don't know about you, but that's the kind of love I want."

Bailey pointed at the posting window as comments began flooding in faster and faster. Narrano's words had clearly struck a chord.

They did with Skyy, too. "Ember," she managed, her own throat a little tight after hearing the quote, "why don't you read a few more thoughts from listeners while I queue up the next song?"

There really wasn't anything to do, but it made it sound like a bigger operation than they really were. Plus, she wanted to give Ember more air time. The listeners liked her, and she loved doing the show.

Bailey leaned closer and scanned the scrolling comments, pointing out which ones Ember should read next. Skyy watched the girls, heads together, working as a team. Maybe she should talk to Big Jerry about adding a new show, one geared to a slightly younger audience and hosted by two teenagers.

The discussion landed solidly on taking risks in love, and Skyy was glad to let Ember lead as she leaned back and contemplated Narrano's words. She always thought she had to trust first in order to find love, but in reality, someone else had to risk everything to love her. And she had to do the same.

Love wasn't about trusting someone, it was about risking everything in loving them. No guarantees, only hope.

As the show progressed, Skyy tried to move the topic to pros and cons and how to avoid bad choices, but the incoming comments weren't going there. Deep down, neither was she. Her voice tightened as she came to a decision.

"I'm going to share something personal. Earlier today someone asked *me* about taking a risk—and if I'd say no."

She cleared her throat and avoided the wide eyes coming from Ember and Bailey.

"I'm going with my gut on this. I—"

CHAPTER 32

Canon sipped from the icy can. He should be drinking something hot, but the orange soda felt more appropriate when listening to Skyy. He wondered if she'd taken one with her and was drinking it now as the song ended and her voice filled his earbuds.

"I'm going to share something personal. Earlier today someone asked *me* about taking a risk, and if I'd say no."

Canon sat up straight in the lounger, the cold breeze forgotten even as he sucked in a lungful. He pressed the left earbud tighter.

Skyy cleared her throat. "I'm going with my gut on this. I—"

A crash blasted through the tiny speakers, and he jerked so hard he nearly fell off the chair. Then a gunshot, shouting, and swearing erupted along with girls screaming. He recognized only one word:

"Gabriel!"

Ten seconds seemed like an eternity as he raced to his bedroom and retrieved his service weapon from the safe. Then he was out the back door and skidding to a stop.

He had no car. The ATV was parked against the house. It still ran, but had a broken front suspension from Skyy's crash.

He reached back inside the house and grabbed the keys off the hook, praying the machine would hold together long enough to get him to Deer Cove. The engine started with a roar, but the machine's throttle was the right hand grip. He couldn't reach it with his left hand and control the steering at the same time.

Gritting his teeth, he slipped his arm out of the sling and leaned forward as far as he could until his hand wrapped around the throttle. Burning pain racked his right side, but he bit through it and twisted the grip. The front tires wobbled crazily as he coaxed the ATV up the driveway. When he got to the main road, he forced himself to stop and pull out his phone. As much as he wanted to get to Skyy, he had two calls to make.

CHAPTER 33

Bailey and Ember spun off the stools one direction and Skyy the other as the man fired a shot through the laptop, splintering its screen. He fisted Olivia's hair, and she flailed and kicked him.

"Stop it or I'll kill them!" He pointed the gun at Bailey, gesturing with the barrel. "Come with me." Bailey stood frozen.

"No," Skyy said, then slowly held her palms out when the gun centered on her chest. The man's finger remained curled around the trigger, and Skyy stopped breathing for a moment. Olivia quit struggling, but her sobs ripped into Skyy. She had to defuse the situation. "How did you find us?"

His twisted laugh echoed in the room, destroying any good looks he might have had. Long, dirty-blond hair trailed below his collar in a stringy mess, matching the color of a bushy goatee. Tattoos covered his right arm in red and black, the details hidden behind the ominous gun. The fact he wore only a T-shirt and no jacket against the cold night told her he was high on something.

"Easy with GPS in every phone," he said. "All my girls have them."

Skyy shuddered at the *my girls,* but nodded, keeping him engaged. Bailey's phone might have led him here, but it had also enabled her to listen to *Night Thoughts* and call Skyy that first time.

"Come on." He gestured to Bailey and began backing toward the open doorway, tugging Olivia by her hair. Bailey took one hesitant step, her gaze bouncing between Gabriel and Skyy.

"The police know who you are," Skyy said, keeping her voice steadier than she felt. "You'll be in more trouble if you take the girls."

"They're mine," he spat.

"Your name is Bradley Farmer, and everyone in the state is looking for you and your gold Porsche Cayenne."

Surprise flitted across his face, but then he laughed again. "Well, then it's a good thing I traded up."

Skyy glanced over his shoulder. Parked at the curb was a dark-colored midsize SUV. It could have been any of a dozen makes and models with similar styling.

"And it's a good time to leave California for good."

She took a step to her left to draw the gun farther away from Bailey and Ember.

Gabriel tracked her as he backed toward the door, tightening his grip in Olivia's hair. Tears ran down the girl's face.

"I came to take these girls back, but now they'll help restart my business—somewhere far away from here."

Skyy bumped a chair. Its legs chattered on the tile, and the noise drew Gabriel's attention. In a flash, Ember lifted a chair and hurled it at Gabriel, rushing him at the same time. He ducked, yanking the screaming Olivia down with him as the chair crashed through a front window.

"No!" Skyy yelled as Gabriel fired again. The shot went

into the ceiling as he fell. Ember leaped and smashed him in the face. He clubbed the side of her head with the pistol and she collapsed.

"Stop! *Stop!*" Bailey yelled. "I'll go." Tears ran down her cheeks as she shuffled toward Gabriel, hands raised. "Just don't hurt them." She looked at Skyy, eyes pleading. Was it for help, or for Skyy to stay down and be safe?

The stench of gunpowder filled the room, and the space rang with the shot. Every fiber of Skyy's body ached to jump the man like Ember had done, strangle him with her bare hands. But she was too far away to do anything.

He backed to the doorway, then through it, keeping the gun trained on Skyy as Bailey followed him to the SUV parked at the curb.

"Both of you in the front," he ordered. Bailey opened the passenger door. Gabriel roughly shoved Olivia in. Bailey followed.

The street was deserted, quiet except for thumping music coming from the Fish Hook down the block. The bar's door was closed against the cold.

A million scenarios ran through Skyy's head as she considered her next move. That Gabriel hadn't shot her meant he probably wasn't a cold killer. Evil, yes, but perhaps somewhat predictable. If she could call the police, maybe they could intercept him before he got on a main highway. At this time of night there wouldn't be many cars on the road. He'd be easy to spot.

But if by some miracle he evaded capture, Bailey and Olivia faced an unimaginable future.

The SUV started. It was pointing toward the Swim Beach, the wrong way to leave town. He'd have to turn around. But Main Street, with its diagonal parking on both sides, was narrow, and the back of Canon's pickup stuck out from where she'd parked on the far side. Rather than do a three-point turn, Gabriel turned left up the side street to go around the block and double back onto Main.

Skyy snatched the truck keys off the bar and raced to where Ember rolled on the floor, moaning and clutching her head.

"Ember?" Blood, bright and red, leaked between her fingers, but she opened her eyes. "Are you all right? I've got to go after the girls."

She nodded. "Go!"

Skyy did. She'd parked in a space across the street when she came into town, so the truck was facing south—just what she needed. She clicked the remote as she ran, unlocking the driver door.

Somewhere out on the lake, a motorboat's engine raced, as if someone were driving full throttle in the night. She jumped into the truck and fumbled to get the key into the ignition of the unfamiliar vehicle. Finally, the engine roared to life. She found the emergency brake release, slammed the shifter into Reverse, and floored the gas pedal. The tires squealed and hopped as the truck backed into the middle of the street. She stood on the brake and shifted into Drive.

There were two side streets coming back into Main from the right. She accelerated, peering over the steering wheel. Which road would he come down, the first or the second? Timing was critical for her plan to work.

The Fish Hook was on the far corner at the first intersection, a single light outside the building's door. But the side street T-ing into Main remained dark. Skyy pressed the gas harder, gaining speed as she blew through the first intersection.

The long block stretched ahead, but she saw lights coming from her right and brightening the next intersection.

Gabriel.

And her girls.

If he reached Main Street and made the turn before she got there, she'd never be able to catch the more nimble vehicle on the lake's winding perimeter road.

Skyy kept her lights off and her foot down and willed the heavy truck faster. There was no time to think about how it would go, just that she had to stop him from taking the girls. The truck flew past storefronts, gaining speed as the headlights on the side street grew brighter.

A horrifying possibility rose. What if it was someone else driving down the street? Someone innocent.

Before she could second-guess her decision, Gabriel's SUV burst from the side street, not slowing as it swung onto Main.

Canon cursed the ATV, hanging on as he squeezed barely 10 miles per hour out of the shaking machine. It was faster than he could run the distance, but it took an eternity to reach DC Coffee.

The front door was open, and glass from a shattered window sparkled across the sidewalk. He pulled to the curb and hopped off just as Ember staggered outside.

"Ember, what—?"

"Gabriel took the girls," she said, holding her head. "We have to go after Skyy." She grabbed his arm and tugged him back to the four-wheeler.

Skyy's truck arrived in the intersection at the same moment as the SUV. Gabriel probably didn't even see her, but for a second she glimpsed the side of his head.

She gripped the steering wheel and held her breath, imagining the girls in the front seat. This could go so wrong. She prayed his body would shield the girls.

The nose of her truck plowed into the SUV's driver door.

Without benefit of a seatbelt, Skyy flew forward, only to be slammed back as the airbag exploded in her face. Her head snapped against the seat back, nearly knocking her out, and her lower half crumpled under the steering wheel, wedging her foot against the gas pedal.

The truck's engine whined, and a horrible clattering vibration rose through the floor mat. Above it all came screeching tires and deforming metal.

CHAPTER 34

SKYY WAS DIMLY AWARE OF THE TRUCK STILL MOVING, SLOWLY rotating clockwise as the screeching back tires and combined momentum of the two vehicles carried them down the middle of Main Street.

Suddenly, the engine quit and the truck rocked to a stop. Her ears were ringing from the shotgun-like bang of the airbag, and she blinked to focus after its punch. The material sagged away from her body, and she began extricating herself from under the steering wheel.

The driver door wouldn't budge when she thrust her shoulder into it, so she climbed across the center console and wrenched the passenger door handle. It swung open, and she slid out head first onto the pavement, rolling onto her sore back to protect her head.

Rekindled pain laced her body, but she pushed it down. A few feet away, the SUV had lodged into the curb. Its driver door was smashed in a good foot, and both side windows were gone. Glass particles crunched under her feet as she rounded the back of the car to the passenger side.

The searing odor of gasoline made her eyes water. She

didn't know which vehicle it was from, but she had to get the girls out.

She yanked open the SUV's passenger door. The deflated side curtain airbags hung in the space like white pillowcases, and she batted them out of her way. "Bailey?"

The girl moaned, clutching her head.

Skyy grabbed her under her arms and dragged her backward out of the car. Olivia stumbled out after them falling to her knees and holding onto the door for balance.

"Olivia! Hold on to me!" The girl got to her feet and held Skyy's waist as they backed away from the wreck.

Inside, Gabriel groaned and turned to the open passenger door. He locked eyes with Skyy as she wrestled the girls away. The car's interior light showed red blood streaming from his nose, another gash higher on his forehead. From the hit she'd given him, he should be dead. Unconscious at the least. The airbags had done their job too well.

He bent sideways, his right hand clutching at something on the floorboard. Then he lifted the object and pointed it at her.

From twenty feet away, the gun looked as deadly as it had in the coffee shop.

There was nothing she could do but get as far away as possible. She dug with her heels, pulling and dragging the girls as the weapon's barrel wobbled, sliding down and away for a moment, then back as Gabriel shook his head. Skyy forced her legs to work.

Twenty-five feet.

How good of a shot was he? He'd hit the laptop, but that was before being in a major accident. And she was a much larger target.

Gabriel's face twisted with hate, and his lips spat blood droplets carried on words she couldn't hear.

She turned away from the gaping car door, from Gabriel, from the gun, and hunched over the girls. He might kill her, but she had to keep Bailey and Olivia safe.

Canon and Ember abandoned climbing back on the ATV when a tremendous crash came from a few blocks down the street. They stood, watching a tangle of metal screeching in the dark, headlights tracking along the buildings.

"Skyy!" Ember began running down the center of the street.

Cradling his arm, Canon followed, then caught up. All he could think of was that Skyy, Bailey, and Olivia were probably somewhere in the wreck.

Each pounding step sent pain radiating across his chest and upper back, but he knew it was faster on foot than taking the ailing machine.

Ember struggled, too, holding her head as she lurched forward. She slowed, then surged with new determination.

Deer Cove had no streetlights, but a few of the businesses had interior lights, porch lights, and signs that cast a dim glow over the roadway. As they neared the wreck, Canon recognized the back of his truck. The front end was smashed into an SUV. He presumed on purpose. That meant—

On the far side, he spotted three forms struggling to get away from the wreck. Ember saw them, too. She changed directions to go around on the right, but tripped and fell.

"Keep going!" she yelled, rolling to her hands and knees.

Canon rounded the back of the SUV and spotted Skyy backing away from the wreck with Bailey and Olivia. She stared back at the wreck, then turned, covering the girls with her body.

In the crushed vehicle, Gabriel pointed a gun at them. His finger was on the trigger.

"No!" Canon yelled. Gabriel's eyes flicked to Canon as the gun discharged.

Then the world erupted.

CHAPTER 35

A CONCUSSIVE *WHUMP*, LIKE A GIANT HAND TO THE BACK, hurled Skyy forward. But instead of a bullet lodging in her spine, the world around flared to near daylight, and a wall of heat rolled over them, searing every inch of exposed skin. Tangled in Bailey's legs, Skyy went down, her forehead smacking the unyielding asphalt.

Stunned, she rolled onto her side, gazing in amazement as Deer Cove's buildings lit up orange, their windows reflecting dancing flames somewhere behind her. The putrid odor of burning hair replaced the smell of fuel, and she feebly slapped at her head, then at Bailey's. The girl was half conscious, moaning.

"Skyy!" Olivia said from Skyy's other side. "The car blew up! We have to get away!"

Olivia was right, but Skyy couldn't move. The flames and buildings spun in dizzying circles, a blur of motion that sent her stomach heaving.

"You go," she managed, clutching Olivia's arm. "Help Bailey." The older girl's leg was under Skyy.

"No!" Olivia tugged at Skyy's arm. "We *all* have to go!"

More heat washed over them like an ocean wave, burning

her skin through her jeans and singeing the hair on her bare arms. Olivia cried out, batting at her hair and clothing.

Someone else was screaming too. A man's voice, high-pitched, pleading.

Propelled by Olivia's desperation, Skyy twisted an elbow under her and levered herself an inch from the growing inferno, but she knew it wouldn't be enough. "Olivia, take Bailey!"

"I won't leave you!" The girl continued to pull on Skyy's arm, and Skyy managed another inch forward.

The cold of the street pressed against her stomach and legs, a cool, tantalizing promise in contrast to the burning on her back. But an unreachable one. She panted against the pavement as she dragged Bailey's dead weight a little further.

Hands slid under Skyy. Big hands, pulling her up and carrying her away from the carnage.

"The girls," she said.

"We've got them," a deep voice replied.

Skyy concentrated on not throwing up as her rescuer carried her from the heat. Somewhere a siren wailed, growing closer, and the sounds of shouting began to overshadow the roaring flames.

After another minute, the man stopped and carefully laid her down on the lawn beside the white chapel. The damp cold nearly had her groaning with relief. She couldn't feel the heat of the fire anymore, but she felt the thump as something exploded.

"That was a tire blowing," the man said.

Skyy squinted up at him. He wore a heavy jacket, but his legs were in pajama bottoms, and his feet were bare. "Who are you?"

"Alex Stone," he said. "AJ's husband."

"How did you know…"

"Canon called us," Stone said. "We brought our boat across. Teal stayed with the baby."

"Canon." She raised her head. "Where is he?"

"I'm here," Canon said. Olivia clutched his side, her arms locked around his waist so tight they could hardly walk. She didn't let go when he knelt beside Skyy and pulled her close. "I saw the gun," he whispered in her hair. "I thought he was going to kill you."

Another man carried Bailey, her body hanging limply. He laid her next to Skyy.

"Bailey," she said, brushing the girl's hair away from her face. "Bailey?"

The girl stirred, squinting her eyes and pursing her lips. "Yeah," she rasped. Her eyes opened, and after a few seconds locked onto Skyy's. "Is Olivia—?"

The younger girl unlatched from Canon and threw herself onto Bailey, crying and hugging her. Between sobs she said, "The cars crashed. Skyy pulled us out, and Gabriel tried to shoot us. Then the cars blew up and we almost burned to death."

Bailey pulled Olivia down, rubbing her back while she sobbed. "Shh. It's okay." She turned her head so she could see the fire.

Past the front of the chapel, flames rose twenty, then surged thirty feet above the wrecked vehicles. Two men emptied handheld fire extinguishers, but the little units were no match for the raging flames. Finally, a fire truck rolled up and partially blocked their view. Its flashing lights reflected off buildings, trees, and overhead wires, lighting up the night even more as men from the volunteer fire department connected a hose and began spraying white foam.

Bailey turned back to Skyy. "Did Gabriel get out?"

Skyy looked to Alex Stone. The quick shake of his head

confirmed what Skyy already knew. The keening screams she'd heard had been Gabriel's as he burned alive in the wrecked car. Along with his gun.

"Good," Bailey said. There wasn't a hint of remorse in her voice. Then she whispered to Olivia. "We'll be okay now."

"Ember's hurt at the coffee shop," Skyy said to Alex. "Someone needs—"

AJ arrived supporting Ember, who was hopping on one leg.

"Skyy!" Ember fell to her knees. "You guys are all right!" She threw herself into Skyy's arms, knocking them both to the grass.

"Ouch."

"Sorry sorry!" Ember said, backing off.

But Skyy locked her arms and pulled her tight. Bailey struggled to a sitting position, and she and Olivia joined Ember in a group hug.

Skyy wrapped her arms around the three girls. Tears stung her eyes, and it wasn't from the noxious smoke flooding the street.

They were her girls, and she was never letting them go.

She cinched her arm around Canon as he joined the huddle.

Five people locked together as one. Near total strangers a few weeks ago, now united more deeply than most experienced in a lifetime.

Skyy looked at Canon, traced the set of his chin, the emotion in his eyes. He was one of the good ones.

She wet her lips, his eyes following the motion. "About your question earlier..."

He didn't say anything, just waited. He was good at that. She smiled.

"I wouldn't have said no."

Skyy moved closer, hesitated, and then brushed her lips across his. He drew her tight, deepening what she started, then breaking it far too soon.

"To what?" he asked.

She leaned her forehead against his, wincing as her bruised skin pressed against him, but breathing him in.

He wasn't being oblivious. No, he was making sure she knew exactly what she was saying.

Our deepest desire is to love and be loved in a way that risks everything.

"To you. To everything."

EPILOGUE

EXCEPT FOR OCCASIONAL FORAYS, THE SUMMER HEAT HAD surrendered to frosty mornings that quickly warmed to spectacular, early October days. Fall rains would come later in the month, but today was blue-sky perfection.

Skyy already missed summer. It had sped by, filled with swimming, hot dogs, watermelon, and boating—exactly as she had imagined. Canon had even convinced them all to go fishing, and Olivia caught the biggest trout. Her picture holding it was on the refrigerator.

"Are you ready, Mom?" Ember stood with Skyy in the tiny foyer outside the interior double doors of the chapel, ready to walk her down the aisle.

"I think so." Then Skyy frowned and turned toward the outside doors. "I don't know. Maybe I should—"

"Mom!"

Skyy grinned and shoulder-bumped her daughter. "Got ya. Just kidding."

Ember blew out a breath. "Don't scare me like that!"

Skyy brushed a wayward strand of Ember's hair behind her ear. She'd redone the dip, deep red tips striking against her natural black. "You look absolutely beautiful."

"Like anyone will even notice me," Ember said. "You're the star today."

"We're both stars," Skyy said. Gabriel's bullet had damaged only the laptop screen, so the entire confrontation at DC Coffee had broadcast live on-air. Within a few weeks, listenership doubled, then doubled again. Big Jerry recently agreed to give Ember and Bailey a shot with a new show geared toward their younger audience. "I'm really proud of you, you know."

"Thanks," Ember said, then she turned and gripped the door handles. "Ready or not, let's go." She opened them wide.

Skyy was ready.

Teal had asked her boyfriend's mom, Rayne Conner, to play keyboard, and music drifted out. The melody was oddly familiar, but the arrangement was completely different from what she remembered.

"That song. Is that…?"

"Sage in Winter," Ember nodded. "Got some other surprises for later."

Everyone stood as Skyy tucked her hand into Ember's arm and stepped into the chapel.

Connie Langworth and the Stone family were in the front row on the bride's side. She'd asked them to sit there since they were the closest she had to family—other than Ember, who was now officially her adopted daughter. A pair of Canon's aunts and uncles and several cousins sat on his side.

Ember's boss, Mark, was next to Old Mike, a man she didn't know personally, but saw often at the coffee shop and around the lake writing in spiral notebooks. The few times Skyy had said hi to him, he'd ducked his head, mumbled, and gone back to writing. Yet here he was.

Irene from Bibs' Beauty Barn took photos with her cell

phone. Skyy had gotten her hair and nails done there this morning.

Sheriff Cabot and his wife stood next to Doc Arnold, and there were many others she recognized from stores and around town.

But Skyy's attention was on the front of the chapel.

Canon Truax stood with his brother, Martin, both dressed in black tuxes. On the opposite side, Bailey and Olivia wore pale yellow bridesmaids' dresses matching Ember's.

"Don't forget to smile," Ember whispered as the professional photographer preceded them down the aisle, snapping picture after picture. When they reached the front, Ember handed Skyy off to Canon and joined Bailey and Olivia.

Canon's tux fit him perfectly from his broad shoulders to his trim waist.

"Wow," she said, running her fingers down the jacket lapel. "You are so definitely a cop hottie."

Martin coughed a laugh, and Canon grinned as he leaned close to her ear. "And you're the most beautiful disc jockey I know, Skyy Delaney."

The minister, Pastor McFarr, stepped forward, interrupting their semi-private moment. Bibs from the Beauty Barn stood beside him and spoke first.

"Well, well, well. Would you look at these two beautiful people," Bibs said. She managed to dwarf the much taller man beside her. While Pastor McFarr wore a conservative black suit, Bibs was draped in a tent-sized lavender robe adorned with red roses. Somehow the outfit worked with her silver and purple-streaked spiky black hair.

As owner of the chapel building, a site of frequent weddings, Bibs was newly and officially licensed by an online ministerial school. She swore it was completely legal before

God and everybody, but agreed to an assistant position today since it was her first ceremony. That didn't prevent her from nearly taking over.

"We are gonna have fun today!"

Pastor McFarr welcomed everyone and began speaking about the importance of marriage, but Skyy's focus was on the man beside her. Storm Lake was a long way from Tucson, Arizona. And that first mile driving out of town in search of Cop Hottie had been a huge risk.

As if reading Skyy's thoughts, Bibs said, "*Our deepest desire is to love and be loved in a way that risks everything.*"

Someone in the audience laughed, and Skyy turned to look. Mark was glancing sideways at Old Mike, who had his head lowered and a big smile on his face. Had the laugh come from him?

She didn't have opportunity to dwell on it, because at that moment the minister called on them to recite their vows and trade rings.

They repeated those familiar words spoken at millions of ceremonies each year. But to Skyy their meaning was forged through experience, and they reminded her of the tenuous link to those things that mattered most.

For better or worse;
For richer or poorer;
In sickness and in health;
Until death do us part.

Life was filled with danger, both physical and emotional, and there was no time to waste.

"We now pronounce you husband and wife," Bibs and Pastor McFarr said in unison. "Canon Truax," Bibs said, "you may kiss this beautiful bride of yours! And, Skyy, you kiss your handsome man right back!"

Skyy leaned in, wrapping her arms around Canon's neck as they kissed.

For a long time.

Long enough for people to start laughing and whistling.

Olivia thrust her bouquet in the air and shouted, "Woo-hoo!" which brought even more laughter and applause.

"I couldn't have said it better, Mr. Truax," she said, smiling against his lips.

"Are you ready to begin this crazy adventure, Mrs. Truax?"

Skyy was more than ready.

As they faced the crowd, she gathered her three girls to her side. It would take months of lawyers and court hearings and paperwork, and probably counseling and arguments and teenage angst. But, for better or worse, Bailey and Olivia would be hers.

No...*theirs*. Hers and Canon's.

Their family of five stood before friends and family while the photographer worked and cell phones clicked.

Then they walked down the aisle side by side.

Yes, Skyy Delaney Truax was ready.

Ready to risk everything.

Night Thoughts

When people come into our lives—even good people—they are inconvenient and disruptive to our routine. Yet, they can bring refreshment, opportunity, change, and love — if we're open.

— V.M. NARRANO

The End

A NOTE TO READERS

Thanks for reading *Night Skyy*!

Would you please consider writing a review at your favorite retailer site? They help other potential readers find great books in this competitive world.

I'd love to hear from you! Tell me what you liked or <gasp!> didn't like, and why. Your feedback will make me a better writer.

I have a great team of test readers and editors, and we work hard to catch every error. If you find one that slipped through, **please let me know**. Just send a short phrase I can search for in the master document.

richbullockwriter@gmail.com

BEHIND THE SCENES: NIGHT SKYY

Did you ever stay up late at night and listen to midnight radio? (Your hours may have varied) Wolfman Jack broadcast on XERB as "The Mighty 1090" out of Hollywood, and Delilah (self-proclaimed "Queen of Sappy Love Songs" — with a weekly audience of 9 million!) *still* listens to callers' often sad stories of love and relationships. She responds with a virtual back rub—and maybe some sympathetic advice.

John Tesh's *Intelligence for Your Life* program intersperses music with fascinating facts about everything from how many germs are in each sneeze, to how to sleep with a partner who snores. However, its daytime broadcast slot isn't nearly as cool as those nighttime shows.

I first listened to the Wolfman with a small, 1950s crystal radio shaped like a rocket ship where the nose cone was the tuning mechanism. Poor reception, a bulky earpiece, finicky tuning, and deliciously clandestine when huddled under a blanket long past my bedtime listening to a disembodied voice far away.

And so was born the concept for Skyy D's *Night Thoughts* show. Gone are the days of crystal radio receivers, and broadcast radio now takes a backseat to all the streaming services available.

Shows are more varied than ever on smartphones and the Internet, but I suspect listeners haven't changed all that much. Those up late at night are still looking for a community to belong to, a forum where they can share thoughts, and a caring, sympathetic friend who won't hold back telling them what's best.

And a sexy alto voice doesn't hurt.

BOOKS BY RICH BULLOCK

Perilous Safety Series

Perilous Cove

Storm Song

Desperation Falls

Glass & Stone Series

Shattered Glass

Glass Revenge

Killing Callie

Lake Effect Series

Night Skyy

Nonfiction

Beyond Us: The Writings of V.M. Narrano

Wild Life: The Writings of V.M. Narrano

The Shortest Book On Marriage

with Sheryl Bullock

ACKNOWLEDGMENTS

Robert Henslin delivered another stellar cover. Rob's design is often the push I need to finish a book. www.rhdcreative.com

My beta reading team: Nancy Bailey, Patricia Bossman, Carol Dickerson, Sis Hammack, Jennifer Haynie, Nita McCoubrey, Linda Murphy, Hannah Prewett, and Cathi Wofford. Their feedback and suggestions are invaluable.

And my wife, Sheryl, who puts up with long absences as I lose myself in my characters and their stories.

BOOK CLUB DISCUSSION QUESTIONS

1. Do you listen to radio hosts like Delilah or John Tesh *Intelligence For Your Life*? Or—back in the day—were you a fan of Wolfman Jack? What is (or was) the appeal of these programs?
2. Perhaps you know someone like Ember who aged out of the foster system. What was it like for them being on his or her own at such a young age?
3. Is there a program in your city, county, or state that provides transition housing and training in preparation for their adult life?
4. How important is chocolate on Valentine's Day?
5. Which character(s) did you like most? Least?
6. If *Night Skyy* were made into a movie, who would you cast in the roles?
7. What themes did you detect as the story unfolded?
8. Do you know cops with a sense of humor?
9. While reading, did you search for the bands and songs Skyy played on *Night Thoughts*?
10. Could you picture Deer Cove and Storm Lake? Where would you go if you visited there?
11. Did you google V.M. Narrano's writings?

12. Where do you think Skyy and Canon will live full-time?
13. What future do you imagine for Ember, Bailey, and Olivia?
14. How did you feel about the ending?
15. Are there questions and topics you hope Skyy will discuss on future *Night Thoughts* shows?

The author would love to hear your answers and is available for live calls to book clubs.

Contact Rich Bullock - richbullockwriter@gmail.com

ABOUT THE AUTHOR

Rich Bullock writes stories of ordinary people put in perilous situations, where lives are changed forever.

Fortunate to grow up in small-town San Luis Obispo, California, he developed an eye for settings that remind people of home. He lives and writes in Redding, California, where on most days he sees Mount Lassen and Mount Shasta.

www.perilousfiction.com

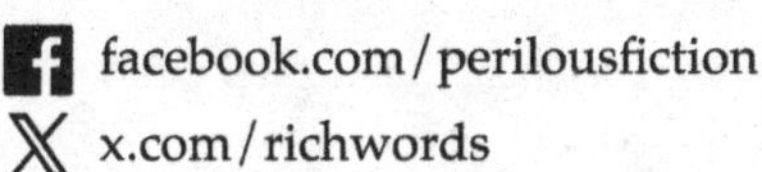

www.ingramcontent.com/pod-product-compliance
Lightning Source LLC
LaVergne TN
LVHW030919080826
845145LV00013B/2962

* 9 7 8 1 9 4 8 1 9 9 0 2 5 *